MR.

60%

CLETE BARRETT SMITH

CROWN
NEW YORK

Text copyright © 2017 by Clete Smith
Jacket art copyright © 2017 by Olga Grlic

All rights reserved. Published in the United States by
Crown Books for Young Readers, an imprint of Random House Children's Books,
a division of Penguin Random House LLC, New York.

Crown and the colophon are registered trademarks of Penguin Random House LLC.

Visit us on the Web! randomhouseteens.com

Educators and librarians, for a variety of teaching tools,
visit us at RHTeachersLibrarians.com

Library of Congress Cataloging-in-Publication Data is available upon request.
ISBN 978-0-553-53466-5 (trade) — ISBN 978-0-553-53467-2 (lib. bdg.) —
ISBN 978-0-553-53468-9 (ebook)

Printed in the United States of America
10 9 8 7 6 5 4 3 2 1
First Edition

Random House Children's Books supports the
First Amendment and celebrates the right to read.

For Jerry Perkins and George Nicholson
(I miss you guys.)

ONE

Matt Nolan kept his head bent low as he walked toward the front doors of the high school. A sophomore stepped in front of him. Matt could see the tip of a fifty-dollar bill clutched in the sophomore's fist.

"Hey," the sophomore said. "I, uh, I heard that you—"

Matt shook his head once. "Not here."

The sophomore stopped. Matt didn't break stride. The sophomore stared for a moment at the money in his hand, then jogged to catch up.

"But I heard that you—"

"Not here." Matt jerked his head in the direction of the security camera mounted over the front doors. He pushed through. The sophomore followed, staying a few paces behind.

Matt wound his way between the tables in the student

commons, settling into a chair in the corner behind a pillar. The sophomore moved to join him.

"Don't sit down."

"Okay." The sophomore shuffled his feet and looked around as the commons filled with students from the morning buses. He thrust the money at Matt. "Here, I—"

"Put that away."

"Okay." He jammed the money into his pocket. "Okay." He shuffled from side to side. "So . . . how do I . . . ?"

Matt kept his gaze on the table. "How much you got?"

"Fifty."

Matt shook his head once. "It's a hundred."

"But I heard—"

"I don't know you. First time's a hundred."

"But I don't have—"

"Then get the fuck away from me."

The sophomore rubbed his palms on his jeans. He glanced over at a table where a group of his friends sat, watching him. "Okay. Okay, a hundred. I've got it. I can get it."

"You will never hand me money." Matt continued speaking to the table. "The john on the third floor. Last stall. That's your spot. Tuck the cash behind the metal casing that holds the toilet paper. Has to be there by noon." It was quiet for a minute. "We're done now."

"Okay. Yeah. But how do I—"

"You'll have it by the end of the day."

Eventually the sophomore drifted away, toward the staircase, looking over at the administrative offices with deliberate casualness.

...

During first period the police officer assigned to the school pulled Matt out of class. Walked right into the middle of Hanoran's Remedial English lecture and called Matt's name. Matt was out of his last-row chair and through the door of the classroom before anyone had a chance to notice he had ever been there. He walked ahead of the police officer through the empty hallways, directing himself to the officer's cubbyhole on the first floor. The officer had to increase the length of his strides to keep up.

Matt dropped his backpack on the table, spread his legs to shoulder width and raised his arms. The police officer patted him down, arms, then torso, then legs from ankle to crotch. Afterward he unzipped the backpack and rifled through the contents.

"You ever get tired of this, Hershey?"

The officer sighed. He zipped up the bag and handed it to Matt. "See you soon."

During sixth period Matt took a bathroom break from Basic Algebra and walked to Mr. Fitzsimmons's classroom on the second floor, past the library storage rooms and the custodial services closet. The nearly retired Fitzsimmons could be counted on to use his prep period to sneak a cigarette break in the teachers' parking lot. He never locked his classroom.

Matt entered the room and crossed to the projector stand in the corner. The projector was coated with a fine layer of dust. It wasn't even plugged into the computer. Matt flipped open a compartment in the back, reached in and withdrew a small ziplock bag. It contained a variety of pills plus a few buds of high-grade marijuana and was known around school as a party bag.

Matt slipped it up the sleeve of his faded sweatshirt.

After school, Matt approached the sophomore in the crowded hallway from behind, paused briefly, then walked on by.

"Hey," the sophomore said. "I've been looking all over for you." Matt stopped and turned. The sophomore had two friends with him. They stared, wide-eyed, at Matt. "So when do—"

"Tell them to leave."

The sophomore's friends needed no further invitation and scurried away. "So when do I get—"

"It's in your backpack."

The sophomore's eyes went wide. "Really?"

Matt didn't answer stupid questions. For the first time, he looked at the sophomore, pinning him down with a stare right in the eyes. "You know what happens if you mention my name to Gill? If you get caught with it?"

The sophomore swallowed. He nodded. Everyone knew what happened if you ratted out Matt Nolan to the vice principal. Some people swore you could still make out the bloodstains in the back parking lot from last year.

Matt turned and walked through the commons and out the front door.

TWO

On the way home from school, Matt stopped by the FeelRite Pharmacy. He had to check each aisle to find what he was looking for.

He tucked the box under one arm and stood at the end of the aisle, peering at the cashier's station, blocked from sight by a revolving stand of used paperbacks. He waited for a Latina woman with four children to finish buying a carry-cart full of medicines and snacks.

When they left, he stepped toward the cashier. An elderly woman came through the front doors then, and Matt stepped back into his hiding place. She fumbled through her purse for a receipt and mumbled something to the cashier, who kept leaning forward to ask her "What?" Matt cursed under his breath.

He scanned the parking lot through the front windows for any more arrivals. He didn't want witnesses.

When the old woman finally shuffled away, Matt approached the cashier and put his box on the counter. The FeelRite Portable Toilet for Adults. The picture on the box looked like an oversized toddler's potty on stilts. Matt laid two fifty-dollar bills on top of the box, his scowl silently daring the cashier to make a smartass remark.

THREE

When Matt walked through the entrance to the trailer park he passed a circle of middle-aged men lounging around a sagging picnic table, empty beer bottles scattered at their feet. One of them shouted to Matt, "Hey, my man. You got any free samples today?" This got a chuckle from the rest of the group.

"Yeah, brother," said someone else, his white tank top yellowed by nicotine and neglect. "I got to tell Unemployment I at least tried lookin' for a job today. You doin' any hiring for your little business?" More laughs.

Matt lifted his head in recognition but just passed on by. He never sold to any of those guys. They were always broke, for one thing, and for another thing, you don't shit where you eat.

The door of the trailer often stuck in the frame and he had to jostle it open. The interior of trailer #6 consisted of a small kitchen/living room, a narrow hallway, a tiny bathroom and one bedroom.

Spilling out of a recliner and sprawled across the coffee table was a man in a bathrobe. Eyes closed, head lying at an odd angle on the table, mouth open and tongue hanging to the side. It was easy to see the shape of his bones wherever exposed flesh peeked through the holes in his bathrobe. He was perfectly still.

Matt ignored the man and walked to the kitchen area. He grabbed a box of Cinnamon Pop-Tarts, put one in the toaster and chewed on another.

The man slowly opened one eye. Matt pretended not to notice. The man closed his eye and began to moan, a guttural sound from deep within his chest.

"That's not funny anymore," Matt said.

The moan rose to a horrible crescendo, melding into a series of exaggerated warbles and gagging noises. When it was over the man opened both eyes and chuckled. "That was my death rattle. How'd you like it?" His toothy grin covered his entire face.

"That's not funny anymore."

"Ah, t' hell with you. You never had a sense of humor."

"When you were two hundred pounds, playing dead was funny, Jack." Matt took the Pop-Tart out of the toaster and bit into it. "Not anymore."

Jack used both hands to smooth down what was left of his red-going-gray hair. He pulled himself up into the recliner. When he got upright a spasm of coughing seized his body. He lowered his head and pounded on his knee until the coughing fit passed, then spat into a dirty ashtray. "You got any smokes?"

"Those things'll kill you."

"Oh, now who's the comedian? Come on, where'd you hide 'em? I'm not so sick I can't still whip yer ass if I feel like it."

Matt balled up his paper towel plate and chucked it in the garbage can. "You couldn't take me in your best days," he said, but he reached on top of the fridge for a pack of unfiltered Camels. He tossed it across the room.

"Thanks," Jack said, lighting up his cigarette with a slightly shaking hand. "Tell me something, when are you gonna bring a girl over here? Don't you think I get tired a just lookin' at you every day? Don't you make any girlfriends at that school?"

"You couldn't handle my girlfriends. If even one of them walked in here all the blood you have left would rush to your dong and you'd drop dead. For real this time."

Jack tilted his head back and blew a stream of blue-gray smoke at the ceiling. "But what a way to go."

The two shared a silence while Jack smoked. Matt drummed his fingers on the kitchen table and took a deep breath.

"Jack? I have something for you, but you're not gonna like it."

"That right? I'm getting a lot of things I don't like lately."

Matt slid the box from the bag and set it on the coffee table. He let Jack read the words for himself.

"Oh, no," Jack said. "No, no. Hell, no." He started to push himself out of his seat but collapsed in another fit of coughing.

When he was finished, Matt said, "Look, just use it at night, okay? Just at night. That's all I'm asking. I'll put it right by your bed."

"Hell, I don't need that." Jack kicked at the box but missed and knocked the ashtray off the coffee table. He swore and rubbed his ankle.

"Dammit, Matt, I still remember when you first used one a them things." Jack suddenly smiled again. "First time, know what you did? I was watching football with a couple a buddies, it's overtime, and you run in hollerin', 'Come look what I done, Uncle Jack. Come look.' You was so proud I thought you must a shit a solid gold brick." Jack's eyes crinkled up and his shoulders shook with laughter. "Hell, you wouldn't shut up until I went and *looked* at it. And don't think I didn't take a load of crap from my buddies, neither. Pun certainly intended."

Jack's shoulders stilled, his smile faded. He shook his head and his sigh drained the rest of the color from his face. "And now you want me to use it?" He looked away from the box, denying its existence with his selective line of vision.

"Just at night," Matt said.

The silence stretched between them. Matt finally stood up, grabbed the box and marched it down the hallway and into the bedroom.

When he returned, Jack said, "You wanna play some cards? Get yer ass whipped by an old man with one foot in the grave and the other on a wet banana peel?" He chuckled, but it was getting harder every day to distinguish between his laughter and the wheezing sound he made after coughing.

"Sure. Let's play."

FOUR

"I've been at this twenty-seven years and you're the most con-
sistent student I've ever seen." Mr. Marsh, the counselor, spread
Matt's first-semester report cards on his desk. "Basic Algebra, 60.3
percent. Earth Science, 60.2. Business English, 61.1. Metal Shop,
60.5. US History, 60.7. It's uncanny. How do you explain it?"

Matt shrugged.

"I'm serious, Matt. How do you manage to exert the abso-
lute bare minimum effort required to pass? In every discipline
we offer?" The silence was heavy and hung there for over a minute. "These are not rhetorical questions."

Matt looked at the desk. "They'll give me a diploma that
looks just like everyone else's."

"Ahhh, not so fast." Mr. Marsh pulled a paper from the top
drawer of his desk. "Not so fast. That's why I asked you to come

see me. The school board passed a new rule last night. You hear about it?"

Matt shook his head. "I don't get to as many meetings as I would like."

"No problem. I have a copy of the minutes right here." Mr. Marsh cleared his throat and read, " 'In an effort to ensure that all students are on a path to well-rounded citizenship after graduation, each senior will be required to join at least one extracurricular club during his or her final year of high school.' "

Matt scoffed.

"Well?" Mr. Marsh said.

"They can't do that."

"They can. They have."

The door of Mr. Marsh's office opened and Vice Principal Gill stuck his head into the room. He looked over Matt's head to the counselor. "Did you tell him?"

Mr. Marsh nodded.

"And is he going to drop out?" Saying it just like that, like Matt wasn't in the room.

"We're getting there, Mr. Gill." Mr. Marsh looked back at Matt. "This rule takes effect immediately, so you need to . . ." Mr. Gill remained in the doorway, watching. Mr. Marsh fixed him with a stare. "Is there anything else I can help you with right now? Or should I get back to the conversation I was having with this student?" Gill glared at Mr. Marsh but shut the door.

Mr. Marsh sighed. "Matt, Mr. Gill there thinks the only reason you show up at school at all is to have access to customers. Even if he can't prove it."

Matt said nothing.

"But at least you're technically passing. And you're right about one thing. If you join a club and keep those grades above sixty percent, you do indeed get a diploma, on official school paper and everything. Does that mean anything to you?"

Matt shrugged.

"I'm serious, Matt. I know it's the biggest cliché in the counselor handbook, but where do you see yourself in five years? What are you going to have to do to get there?"

Thinking about the future was like staring into a dark cave. Matt remained silent.

Mr. Marsh sighed. "I checked out all the clubs. And I mean all of them. There's only one that you're qualified to join, especially at this late date. Helping Hands. It's a community service club. They meet in room 212."

Matt gave no indication that he'd heard.

"They meet every Tuesday, next meeting's tomorrow. If you want to stay in school, start attending. And just between you and me, I'm sure Gill will be there to take attendance."

"Can I go now?"

Mr. Marsh opened a green file folder on his desk. "That's it, Matt? 'Can I go now?' That's the best you got? I know there's more in there than Mr. Sixty Percent."

"Can I go now?"

Mr. Marsh exhaled slowly and scooped up Matt's report cards. "Sure. Why not?"

Matt pushed himself out of the chair and reached for the doorknob.

"One last thing," Mr. Marsh said, taking another piece of paper out of Matt's file. "Is there someone at your place I can talk to? It says here you live with your grandmother. Maybe I'll give her a call."

Matt shook his head. "No need."

"What does that mean?"

"I'll be there. Tomorrow."

FIVE

Matt awoke to crashing and cursing from the dark hallway. He pushed away the unzipped sleeping bag and tumbled off the couch. The clock on the TV read 2:17. He flicked on the hallway light.

Jack lay sprawled face-first on the carpet, halfway between the bedroom and the bathroom. Without the bathrobe, it looked like his shoulder blades could slice right through the skin on his back. A brown stain covered the seat of his boxers and spread down his legs.

Jack struggled to stand up, wisps of his thinning hair sticking up in all directions. He slipped and fell again. Matt rushed to him, grabbing him under the armpits and hauling him up. "Lemme go," Jack mumbled. "Myself. Do it myself." He climbed up on shaky legs, his half-opened eyes cloudy. He tottered and nearly fell over backward but reached out to clutch at the wall for support.

"Have to clean you up," Matt said. Jack was now facing the wrong way, toward the bedroom. Matt reached to take him by the elbow and lead him into the bathroom.

"Goddammit, I do it myself," Jack said, louder now, and he wheeled around and threw a feeble forearm punch that grazed Matt's shoulder.

The smell of Jack's mess hit Matt then, triggering his gag reflex. He lunged for the bathroom to vomit in the toilet but wasn't entirely successful with his aim. He rinsed his mouth out in the sink, threw a towel over the puke that had hit the floor, then turned on the hot water in the bathtub.

Jack stood in the doorway, his eyes a little more alert. "I'm all wet. What the hell's going on?" He reached behind himself and his hand came away covered in excrement. That woke him up some more. "Ah, hell . . . shit, this is wrong . . . this is all wrong." He leaned against the doorjamb and shook his head. He held his hand as far away from himself as he could, a foreign artifact he didn't know how to get rid of. "Hell, I don't . . . I'm sorry."

"Just don't touch anything. Get in the tub." Jack fumbled with his boxers for a long time with his left hand before he was able to shuffle them off. Matt grabbed a corner of the boxers between thumb and index finger and dropped them in the trash. "Next time, you're using that goddamn port-a-potty."

"I thought I could—"

"Just get in the tub."

Matt helped Jack climb into the puddle of warm water. Jack

quickly slumped against the side of the tub and started snoring, his mouth stretched wide open.

By the time Matt got Jack back into bed and cleaned up the bathroom and the mess in the hall it was past three-thirty. He didn't sleep the rest of the night.

SIX

Mr. Gill was waiting outside room 212, arms folded across his chest, when Matt approached after school. The vice principal grunted and looked at his watch. "So you decided to show up."

Matt waited for Gill to step aside but the man continued to block the door. Matt stood there, staring at the lockers lining the halls.

"You're really going through with this?" Mr. Gill said. "You know you have to be at every single meeting? On time. And you have to actually work on something, not just sit there like you do in class. One screw-up and you're out, understand? Out of my school."

Mr. Gill's high forehead reddened. "Hel-*lo*? Are you even listening? Look at me. I said look at me." Matt shifted his gaze from the lockers to Mr. Gill's chest. His eyes were bleary from sleep deprivation. "Good lord. You been smoking that stuff already today? No wonder your grades are in the toilet."

Mr. Gill turned and propped open the door. Matt watched him enter but stayed in the hallway.

The desks in room 212 had been rearranged to form clusters of three or four students each. The room was noisy, each group of teenagers discussing individual projects. Ms. Edwards, the club's advisor, sat at her desk at the front, working on her computer. She stood when Mr. Gill entered. "May I help you?"

"I have a new member for your club." Mr. Gill motioned to Matt, who took one step closer to the doorframe but remained in the hall. "Let's go," Mr. Gill barked. "If you're going to do this then get in here." Matt took another half-step forward, pausing in the doorway. The clamor of many conversations died down.

"Oh," Ms. Edwards said. "I see. I'm . . . I'm afraid our committees are rather full at the moment." She cleared her throat. "Are you sure Helping Hands . . . is the best . . . opportunity?"

Matt looked up from the floor for one second to scan the classroom. He had sold party bags to over half of the students in here.

"He's your new member," Mr. Gill said. "I'll check in next week. Gotta run. Big meeting with District." He left the room.

"Well," Ms. Edwards said. She smoothed her skirt. "Well. I suppose we'll need to find you a committee, then." The other students averted their eyes, restarted their discussions at half volume, pushed their circled desks slightly closer together. Ms. Edwards opened her mouth, then closed it. She picked a piece of paper off her desk and managed to find her smile again. "Okay,

Matt, so this is a list of all the committees and a description of their projects. This will give you some idea of what Helping Hands is all about." She handed the paper to him and waited a few moments before he took it from her. "You could always start your own project?" She looked hopefully at Matt, who said nothing. "Or . . . maybe you could pick one of these and we'll see if there's room?"

Matt gripped the paper, his eyes flying over the words without reading them. He could feel the heat of stolen glances all over his body, like the red pinpricks of light from laser gunsights he had seen in countless action movies on late-night basic cable. It took more willpower than he knew he possessed to stay standing in front of that room.

He was close to bolting, damn the consequences, when a girl in the back raised her hand. Hers was the only single desk in the room, alone in the corner. "Ms. Edwards? Matt can join my committee."

Ms. Edwards stopped fiddling with her skirt. She took the paper out of Matt's hands. "That's an excellent idea. Why don't you join Amanda?"

Matt shuffled over and sat at a desk, scrunching himself below the gaze of two dozen pairs of eyes, and felt like he could breathe again.

"I guess it's not technically a committee if I'm the only member, though, huh?" the girl said, casting a quick glance at the people surrounding them. "So it's a good thing you showed up."

Matt looked at the clock.

"Oh, my apologies. I should introduce myself. I'm Amanda," the girl said. "We've had a couple of classes together but never officially met."

Matt didn't recognize the girl. Her body was fat in a way that defied polite euphemisms. Matt had no idea that you could buy a pink sweatshirt with Disney characters on it in that large of a size. It seemed like it belonged on a much smaller person, a little kid, which made the look even worse.

Her face was covered by a smile that crinkled up her eyes. She extended her hand. It took Matt a few moments to figure out he was supposed to shake it.

Amanda scooched her desk over to be closer to Matt's. She gestured to some papers and a calendar on her desktop. "I'm in the middle of organizing a children's book drive for the hospital," she said. "A special collection for the kids who have to stay overnight. The stuff in the waiting room always gets so torn up."

Matt nodded once.

"I got the idea from my mom," Amanda said. "She works nights at the hospital and sometimes has a shift in the children's wing. Some of those little guys could really use some cheering up."

Matt traced a name that had been carved into his desk.

"I remember in third grade, I had to have my appendix taken out," Amanda said. "Boy, I was so nervous in that hospital bed I couldn't sleep all night. Hopefully we'll be able to help kids just like that."

Amanda waited politely during the times when it would have been Matt's turn to speak, just like they were having a real conversation.

"The planning stage is pretty much over," she said. "I've done the publicity and contacted donors in the neighborhood. Now the books just need to be picked up and taken to the hospital."

Matt could feel the stares again, people looking in his direction from every corner of the room. Someone from the nearest group half-whispered, "Perfect match. One sells the weed and the other gets the munchies." Laughter was poorly concealed behind hands or disguised as coughs.

"Assholes," Matt muttered to himself. He glanced at Amanda. Her smile had slipped a bit. She studied her hands, folded on top of the desk. "Those people are assholes," Matt told her.

Amanda lifted her head. "Usually the people here are really nice," she whispered. "Especially in a club like this. Most of them really want to help other people."

"Most of them are resume whores."

Amanda shook her head. "I don't believe that."

Matt shrugged. Amanda bent her head and filled out paperwork.

After a while Matt said, "So no one else is on this committee?"

"No, it's just me. I prefer to work alone," Amanda said. "But I don't mind if you join," she quickly added. "I'm at the stage where I could use a little help, actually. There are a lot of boxes of books to be picked up."

Matt shook his head. "I don't have much time. Gill said it was just Tuesday afternoons. Meetings."

"Ms. Edwards lets us sign in here during meeting times and then leave campus to do the legwork," Amanda said. "Does that work for you?"

"Guess it'll have to."

SEVEN

The rest of the week was surprisingly smooth. Matt added a new in-house stash behind some loose paneling in the locker room and adjusted his money drop-off sites with some regulars. Business was good.

It remained embarrassingly easy to get by in his classes. Matt had learned long ago that if he showed up and sat at a desk, turned in the thinnest of half-assed attempts when assignments were due, kept his mouth shut and avoided discipline problems, no teacher in the school would fail him.

And Jack. Jack hadn't had a screaming pain fit in over a week. Matt thought he had finally figured out the right medicine cocktail to keep Jack at least semicomfortable: the morphine he got from Big Ed for the pain, a triple shot of Benadryl to help him sleep and a little bit of Matt's weed twice a day to get his appetite up. Although the only things he would agree to eat were rocky road ice cream and frozen fish sticks dipped in barbecue sauce. Matt couldn't believe how little Jack ate some days.

Jack was better in the evenings. More clearheaded, more energy. They were able to play cards, sometimes for almost two hours at a stretch. Cribbage, five bucks a point. They kept a running tally of the totals. So far Matt owed Jack $32,795.

And Matt was able to worry a little less when he had to leave the trailer. He had rigged up a timer system, a stopwatch that he set to beep every four hours. That way Jack would remember to take his medicine when Matt was at school or out on business. It had been eight gloriously peaceful days since Jack had forgotten.

For the first time in months Matt felt like he was almost able to keep up with things. Like he wasn't buried in it the second he woke up in the morning.

It lasted until Friday. His burner cell phone vibrated in his pocket in the middle of fourth period. He checked the number underneath his desk. It was Janice, the trailer park manager. Not good.

Matt grabbed a bathroom pass and slipped out the classroom door. He heard some wiseass whisper, "Oh, I wonder where he's going," to some other wiseass.

Matt ducked into the stairwell and returned the call.

"Yeah?"

"It's Matt. You called?"

"Yeah. About Jack. I really don't have time for his shit right now." The smacking of Janice's gum was louder than her words.

"What'd he do?"

"Shit, kid, what didn't he do? You need a get down here and corral him, right away."

Matt looked at his watch and swore. Gill was just waiting for the chance to nail him, build up enough offenses in his file to run him out. "Can't you just tell him to sit in the trailer and wait until I get home?"

"We're way past that point. Yer not here in ten minutes and I'm callin' the cops. You don't want that, right?"

"I'll be there as soon as I can."

Matt was panting heavily from running all the way to the trailer park.

"Hot damn, kid, he's in fine form today," one of the picnic table regulars called to Matt as he rushed by.

"What you feedin' him for breakfast, anyway?" shouted another.

Matt saw Jack down at the end of a row of trailers. He was beating on the rusted siding of trailer #11 with a big stick. Matt had no idea where he had gotten that much energy.

Matt could hear Jack ranting as he got closer, barking and wheezing to the park at large. "Who took it?" Jack said, emphasizing the words with a *bang* of the stick on the trailer. "Which one a you bastards took it?" *Bang. Bang.* "I ain't goin' away till I find ya." *Bang.* "I'm gettin' it back, then I'm gettin' the hell outta here." *Bang.*

Jack set his feet shoulder width apart and wrapped both hands around the base of the stick, baseball batter style, to take a bigger cut at the trailer. He uncorked a hefty swing and missed, stumbling to an awkward rest on one knee. He pushed himself up, using the stick for support. The stick was being shakily raised to shoulder level for another home run swing when Matt reached him.

"What the hell are you doing?" Matt ripped the stick from Jack's hands and tossed it aside.

"Huh?" Jack turned and his knees buckled. Matt caught him around the chest and shoulders before he crumpled to the ground.

A woman's face appeared above them in the tiny bathroom window of trailer #11. "About time!" came the shrill voice through the dirty screen. "He hit my trailer again and I would've come out there myself. He's been terrorizing the whole neighborhood."

Matt waved at the window and pulled Jack toward trailer #6. Jack's shoulders felt bird-thin, breakable. Matt had sat atop those shoulders as a boy, even when he was way too old for it, getting rides to the Quik-N-EZ Mart for a Freezy Drink. It had seemed like miles but Jack always hauled him there the whole way. And back. Even when Matt dribbled grape Freezy on his head. It was hard to believe those were the same shoulders.

"Lemme go," Jack mumbled. His energy was gone, feet barely dragging through the gravel as Matt lugged him home.

"What in the hell were you doing?" Matt spoke in hushed tones, intensely aware of the hidden eyes watching them from the surrounding trailers.

"Someone stole my car," Jack said. He found enough steam

to raise his voice and jab his finger at the row of trailers. "One a these low-rent bastards stole my car and one of us hadda be man enough to get it back." He paid for his half-shout with a coughing jag.

"Jesus," Matt muttered. He shook his head.

Jack spat out a brown glob. "What's yer problem?"

"We sold that car. Six months ago."

"Why in hell'd we do that?"

"To pay the fucking doctor bills. And get started on a supply of morphine. Don't tell me you don't remember that. You wanna go back to the way it was before the morphine?"

Jack shoved himself away from Matt's arms. Matt fully expected him to fall in a heap, but Jack found a shaky balance and plodded the last few feet to the trailer, where he wrestled unsuccessfully with the door.

Janice approached from her manager's office a few trailers down. "Everything under some kind a control?" She flicked the ash from her cigarette into a puddle.

Matt nodded. He struggled for a moment to find the right words. "Look, I'm glad you called me instead of the cops," he said.

"Whatever. Just make sure he stays under wraps." She turned and walked back to her office.

Matt pushed Jack aside and forced the trailer door open, then stepped away and gestured for him to enter.

"You shouldn't a sold that car," Jack said, and pulled himself through the door.

EIGHT

Jack collapsed on the couch while Matt stalked down the narrow hallway to the bathroom. He flicked on the light. "Oh, great," he muttered. "This is exactly what I need right now."

The grimy countertop was covered in pills, tubes and over-turned canisters. Matt was horrified to see much of their dwindling supply of morphine—those precious peace-bringing blue tablets—scattered in the sink. A few of them were half-dissolved in stray drops of water; others clung in a little circle around the drain. Some of them had obviously fallen through. Matt carefully scooped up as many as he could and dropped them into the proper canister.

There were other medicines mixed in the mess, aspirin capsules and cold remedy gelcaps and dull pink dots of Pepto-Bismol. It looked like Jack had ripped apart the entire medicine cabinet.

Then Matt saw the NeverSleep wrapper on the warped lino-leum floor. *Extra Energy!* it promised. *For Those On the Go All Nite!* He had bought those recently to help out on the school days that followed a tough night with Jack. He picked up the packet and looked in. There were many more pills missing than he had taken. He shook his head, staring at the packet in his hand.

The medicine timer beeped then, promptly sounding at its appointed time. Matt snatched it up and smashed it against the countertop in one fluid motion. He tossed the mechanical car-cass into the wastebasket.

He marched down the hall to the living room. "Did you take these?" He held the NeverSleep wrapper in the air.

"What if I did?"

"Why in hell would you take these, Jack? You need your rest. You know that."

"Fuck my rest."

"You can't combine these with other meds. You went crazy on the entire trailer park. Where we gonna go, they kick us out?"

"Fuck my rest, and fuck you. Sometimes a man's gotta get up. Get outside." Jack grabbed the blanket from the back of the couch and threw it in a heap on the floor.

"Whatever. You know what? Take as many as you want." Matt tossed the NeverSleep packet on the coffee table. "I'll just lock your ass in whenever I have to leave. I'll find you a special stick and you can beat the hell out of the walls all you want." He stepped into the kitchen area and opened the fridge even though he wasn't hungry. He grabbed a package of baloney and a nearly empty mustard jar, then a loaf of bread from a cupboard, just to have something to do to keep his hands from shaking.

Matt sat at the tiny kitchen table, chewing his tasteless sandwich and staring at his paper towel plate. Jack sat on the couch, arms crossed, staring at the blank TV screen. They were quiet for a long time.

"You wanna know why I took them pills?" Jack said. Matt looked up from the table and nodded once. "You gotta promise not to laugh, you hear me?" Matt looked at his uncle. "You gotta promise."

"I'm not exactly in a laughing mood. Shoot."

"I been having this dream. Can't shake it." Jack ran a hand over his thinning hair. Took a deep breath and let it out in a long, trembling sigh. "I have it most every time I fall asleep now. And it's always the same." He slowly shook his head. "I was watching TV and felt myself losing it, going under. That's when I pulled myself up and looked through the bathroom for those pills. I . . . I can't explain it . . . but there's just no way I could face that dream again. Not right away."

The two were quiet for a few minutes. Matt shuffled over to the fridge, scooped up a spoonful of rocky road ice cream and set the bowl on the coffee table in front of Jack, then sat at the kitchen table. "What's the dream about?"

Jack stared at the wall. Matt didn't think he was going to

say anything, but he eventually started talking. "It's nighttime. Pitch-black. I'm sittin' at the wheel of a car." Jack's eyes seemed to sink into their sockets. Matt could tell that he no longer saw the inside of the trailer, that he was caught up in his dream world. "At first there's streetlights and some roadside stuff, you know, a billboard with a hot girl on it or a restaurant or some damn thing. But pretty soon all that gives out, and it's just a long stretch a dark road. Big guardrails on either side, up above the roof a the car."

Jack shuddered. He absentmindedly passed a hand over his forehead, wiping at beads of sweat. "It just—The damn thing goes on and on, you know?"

Jack got quiet for a long time. Matt wasn't sure he wanted to hear the rest. But the slack-jawed look creeping over Jack's face was even worse. "Is that it?" Matt asked.

Jack blinked heavily and shuddered again. He took another deep but shaky breath and continued. "After a while I jam my foot on the brakes, but nothing happens. Car keeps cruising. I grab the . . . the . . ." Jack mimed holding a circle in front of him but couldn't find the words. Jesus, he was losing it today.

"The steering wheel?" Matt sighed.

"Right, I grab at the wheel and try to turn things around, but all I can do is swing the car from side to side." Jack's body swayed slightly at the remembered motion. "Pretty soon I get scared, not just dream-scared but honest-to-shit scared, and I swing the wheel back and forth, ramming the car into those guardrails." Jack got quiet again. He squinted, looked into the middle distance, maybe sizing up those phantom guardrails.

When he spoke again, Matt could barely hear him. "But I can never bust through 'em. Just keep bouncing off and back onto the road."

Matt never knew what to say. "That's messed up."

Another too-long silence before Jack responded. "But after that is the worst part." Jack leaned forward in his seat. "'Cause after that the steering wheel stops working. Just gives out. The car's in the dead center of that road, just flyin' along. It's like I got no control over where I'm headed. No control at all."

Jack's shoulders slumped. His eyes returned to the trailer. To now. "I suppose that sounds pretty stupid to a kid like you."

Matt looked around at the tiny living room and low ceiling of the trailer. The muffled laughs and catcalls of the picnic table regulars outside made their way into the living room. He shook his head.

NINE

Matt arrived at the Helping Hands meeting room early and found Amanda alone.

"Hi," she said. "It's nice to see you."

Matt gave a half-wave. Amanda held up a piece of paper. "I put together a map for us. It has all five of our pickup locations for the day. I figured it would help save us some time so we have a chance to drop our first shipment off at the hospital. I can't wait! We might even have time to read a few books out loud to some kids."

"Yeah, about that, look . . ." Ms. Edwards entered the classroom carrying a stack of papers. A few students followed and took their seats. Matt dropped himself into a desk near Amanda and lowered his voice. "I need to be here until what's-her-name takes attendance. Then I gotta run."

Amanda busied herself with the map, hunched over it and retraced the color-coded routes.

Matt watched as students filled up the room, the murmur of overlapping conversations growing louder. He looked at the top of Amanda's head.

"Look, I have this meeting and I can't miss it. I'm pretty sure I'll be able to help next week."

"It's okay," Amanda said without looking up. "Really. I had planned on doing this myself, anyway. It's fine."

The room filled up. Ms. Edwards went over the off-campus rules and took attendance. Matt put his name on the sign-out sheet and slipped out of the room.

Matt walked through the parking lot, zigzagging between the parked cars. It was the best way to avoid being noticed from the front windows of the school. He was nearly to the exit when Hershey pulled up beside him in the police cruiser. "Hold up, there, Matt," he said. "I've got someone wants to talk with you." Hershey put his walkie-talkie to his mouth and pressed a button. "Mr. Gill. Officer Hershey here. Got Matt Nolan in the student parking lot. Near the exit."

A burst of static, then Gill's voice. "I'll be right there."

Matt checked the time on his phone, then crossed his arms. Even staring at the ground it was hard to miss the looks his classmates gave him as their cars funneled by on their way out of the lot.

Hershey tapped a rhythm on the steering wheel. "Look on

the bright side, Matt. A few more months and you'll be gone from here."

An unintelligible jeer came from one of the cars.

"Don't you get tired of this, Hershey? Coming to high school every day?"

Hershey chuckled. "You kidding? A guy like me, married, two kids, this is the sweetest position on the force. There's even a waiting list for it. Regular hours, no weekend work, no getting bumped to night patrol, no showing up in court on your day off. Life is good."

Matt was silent. He crossed his arms, looking up to see Mr. Gill jogging to them from the front door of the school.

Hershey's smile faded. "Look, try not to rile him up too much, okay? I got better things to do."

Matt grunted. Gill drew closer, stopping cars with an upraised palm to cut straight through the lot.

"This school job is a one-year stint for me. I'll be back on the streets next year," Hershey said. "And I don't want to find you there, Matt. Because the rules will be different then, understand? I won't be taking you to detention. Do you understand that? When we meet next year everything will be different. You don't want that, either."

Matt stared into the middle distance, waiting for Gill.

"I know you don't want that." Hershey sighed. "You'll understand, all right, but I'm afraid it'll be too late by then."

Mr. Gill approached the police cruiser, breathing deeply to catch his wind. Finally, he said, "So where are you headed? I thought this was Tuesday. This better be good or we'll be going back to my office to start the paperwork that removes you from this school."

Matt had nothing to say. Gill and Hershey both stared at him. The student cars continued to pass by, loud bass pumping through open windows.

Gill crossed his arms over his chest and shook his head. "Well, this little social experiment didn't last long, did it?" he said to Hershey. "I am so surprised that Mr. Nolan couldn't stick with an extracurricular activity." He turned to Matt. "Get in the car. Officer Hershey will make sure you get back to my office. I've got a few important things to do and then I'll deal with you."

Matt set his jaw and swallowed bitter words. He reached for the door handle.

"Hey, Matt, I've been looking all over for you." All three heads turned to the ancient metallic-gold Buick Electra, an oversized boat of a car, as it pulled up beside Hershey's police cruiser. Amanda was at the wheel. She was blocking the exit and the students behind her honked their horns. "Climb in. We're supposed to be at the first pickup spot by two-forty-five."

Matt looked at Gill and Hershey and saw the same look of confused surprise that must be on his own face.

Amanda's smile was big enough for all of them. "Hi, Mr. Gill. Hi, Officer Hershey. Matt and I are going to pick up children's books for Helping Hands."

"Yes. Yes, of course, I see," said Gill. "Is that . . . I mean, does that . . ."

"We're both officially signed in with Ms. Edwards. She lets us work off-campus during the club meeting times."

Matt opened the door and slid onto the vinyl bench seat next to Amanda.

Gill ducked his head to look into the car. He hadn't quite managed to get the shock out of his eyes yet. "Is that . . . Are you sure everything is okay?"

"You bet," Amanda said. "We're dropping the books off at the hospital for kids. We'll be sure to take plenty of pictures for the school's blog. Wish us luck!"

Amanda's smile was so disarming that Gill actually said, "Good luck," as they drove away.

TEN

"Sorry about the mess," Amanda said, pushing a pile of stuffed animals onto the floorboards, tossing some onto the backseat. "I don't ever have . . . I mean, it's usually just me."

"No problem," Matt said, watching the school buildings and the baseball fields roll by through the car windows. He clutched the door handle. "Thanks. You know, for helping me ditch Gill. Once we get around this corner you can drop me off."

They were silent for a minute. Amanda eased the big car into a grocery store parking lot. Matt's door was half open before the car came to a stop.

When Matt stepped out Amanda said, "You don't have to go." He turned and looked at her. "I could drive you to your meeting and then—"

"You don't wanna do that."

"—and then after, you could help me pick up the boxes of books and take them to the hospital. I actually could use some help with that part. I know it's hard to believe, but I don't really lift weights very often."

Matt scanned the parking lot.

"That was a joke," Amanda said. "You don't smile that much, do you?"

"The meeting's on the other side of town. Over by the bay."

"It's okay. I've got time. And there's even a few pickup spots over by there. Maybe we could stop on the way." Matt drummed his fingers on the roof of the Buick. Amanda waited. "Well?"

"I'm not going into any hospital."

"Okay . . . well, how about just into the lobby? They'll have somebody to help me from there."

Matt waited another minute and then ducked back into the car. Amanda touched the key in the ignition, then let her hand fall away. "There's just . . . there's one more thing, I guess."

"What?"

Amanda's cheeks went pink. "It's, you know, about your meeting. I totally don't mind taking you over there, but I, you know, I mean I can't risk having any . . . stuff . . . in my car."

"Stuff?"

Amanda gripped the steering wheel, looking through the windshield. "You know, stuff. Just about everyone at school . . . I mean, they know what you do."

Matt shook his head. "Whatever." He pushed the door open again and stepped out.

"No, wait! That came out wrong. It's just that I . . ."

"What?" Matt ducked his head to get a look at her.

"Never mind, it'll sound stupid to you."

Amanda opened her mouth, then closed it again. "I don't have time for this," Matt said.

"I applied to nursing school." Amanda's tone was hushed, a confession. "I haven't heard back yet. Please don't tell anyone."

Matt snorted. "Right. Who'm I supposed to tell?" *And who would care?*

"Anyway, I really want to get in. If we, you know, get pulled over or something and they find any stuff it could hurt my chances. Even if it's not mine." Amanda pried her gaze from the windshield and looked at Matt. "I'm not trying to be mean, I swear. Do you still want a ride?"

Matt fell back into the seat and swung the door shut. "Don't worry. I'm not going to ruin your life in one afternoon."

ELEVEN

When Amanda rang the doorbell, the door opened halfway and a
middle-aged woman peeked out. The woman saw Matt standing behind Amanda and pulled the door closer, only her head
and shoulders showing now, and said, "May I help you?"

"Hello, Mrs. McIntire? I'm Amanda, from the high school.
I called about the book drive?"

The woman smiled. "Oh! Of course. Come right in." The
door opened onto a living room with floor-to-ceiling windows
that overlooked the water. The room had enough space for two
#6 trailers.

"This is my friend Matt."

"Nice to meet you both. Can I get you any refreshments,
maybe something to drink?"

"Oh, that's okay," Amanda said. "Thanks for the offer, but

we should probably just pick up the books. We're kind of on a schedule today."

"Of course." The woman turned and walked down a hallway. "Come right this way. The books are in my daughter's room."

On the short walk Matt saw dozens of vases and crystal knickknacks, any one of them probably worth enough money for a three-month supply of morphine tablets.

The woman spoke over her shoulder as she glided across the thick rugs in the hallway. "It's so great that you're doing this. I'd love to find the time to volunteer myself, but you know how it is. Always a million things to do." The woman snuck a peek at a mirror in passing and brushed her hair back with one hand.

They reached a bedroom where a girl sat in bed, propped up by a mound of pillows, playing video games on a big-screen TV. "My daughter Samantha stayed home sick from kindergarten today, I'm afraid." The girl glanced at the visitors and returned to her game. "The boxes are just there. You'll have to lift them, though—they're simply too heavy for me."

"He's the muscle." Amanda pointed at Matt and smiled.

"He certainly is," the woman said.

Matt picked up the boxes, and when he passed by the bed the girl shrieked, "Mom!" Matt flinched, nearly dropping the box. "You can't give away all of those!"

The woman cleared her throat, smiling an apology at Amanda. Her voice was careful, controlled. "But we've discussed this, dear. These books are going to the hospital."

"But, Mom—"

"Charity work is very important." The woman's voice got

louder. She gave Amanda a sheepish glance, then cleared her throat once more and began again, calmer now. "Stop behaving this way, please. You still have lots of other books. These are going to the hospital."

"Not *all* of them," the girl said. She got up on her knees and snatched the book on top of the box. "Not this one." She grabbed the next few books. "And not these, either."

The woman looked nervously from Matt to Amanda, wringing her hands. Matt was a statue.

Amanda sat on the bed and looked at the book in the girl's hands. "*A Fish out of Water.* Boy, I used to love that book when I was really young."

"Me too," the girl said, pulling the book close to her chest.

"My mom used to read it to me every night. My favorite part is when Otto grows bigger and bigger and bigger and pretty soon he doesn't even fit into the swimming pool."

"Did you like that part because you're so big?"

Mrs. McIntire's eyes went wide and she sucked in her breath, but Amanda just shrugged. "Probably. I was pretty big even when I was little." She laughed. "Okay, that came out wrong, but you know what I mean."

"How did you get so big?"

Mrs. McIntire marched to the bed. "*Samantha!* Don't you—"

But Amanda waved her off. "I'll tell you how I got so big." She leaned into the girl, looking left and right to check for imaginary eavesdroppers. "But you can't tell another living soul, okay?" Samantha's eyes went round, and she nodded. Amanda leaned closer still and stage-whispered, "I loooove cupcakes."

The girl squealed with laughter. "I love cupcakes, too!" Amanda mimed eating a huge cupcake, and Samantha joined her.

Amanda sat up, wiped imaginary crumbs from her shirt and held her hand out for the book. "May I?" Samantha handed it over, and Amanda flipped through the pages. "Yep. I think this was the hardest one for me to give up, too."

"What do you mean?"

"I still had all the books from when I was a kid. I never thought I could let go of them, but when I started asking other people to donate books for kids in the hospital, I figured I should probably do the same. But I totally understand if you're not ready yet. You probably still read this one all the time."

Matt shifted his grip on the boxes. They were getting pretty heavy.

The girl looked at the book. "So . . . what happens to the books?"

"Sometimes kids get so sick that they have to stay in the hospital overnight, for an operation or something. These books will be in the overnight rooms for them, maybe make them feel a little bit less scared." The girl chewed on her lip. "You know what made it easier for me to let go of them?"

"What?"

"I realized that if I gave the books away, I would still have my great memories from them. Nothing could take those away. Because the love isn't in those pages, it's in me. Does that sound weird?"

Samantha shook her head.

"I know I'll miss them, but I think about how happy some

other little girl will be, and that makes it easier." Amanda handed the book over and stood. "But I totally understand if it's too soon to give these up. Do you want to go through the boxes and see how many you want to keep? Or should we just leave all of them?"

Samantha thought for a moment. "It's okay. You can take them all."

"Are you sure?" Amanda said. "I meant it when I said I understand if it's too soon."

"No, it's okay. I don't really read those much anymore. The little kids at the hospital can have them."

"Great," Amanda said. "Thanks a lot, Samantha. You're awesome." Samantha beamed back at her.

Mrs. McIntire ushered them to the front door. "I'm so sorry for her behavior," she said. "Sometimes I just don't know what to do with her."

"It's fine," Amanda said. "I really like kids. Thanks so much for helping us out with the book drive."

Matt followed her out the door.

TWELVE

Matt knocked on the door of the rambler and waited several minutes. He glanced at the surrounding houses. Tidy lawns, new paint jobs, fenced-in backyards. He tried to even out his breathing, to quiet the little voice that said *You don't belong here.*

Big Ed opened the door. "You back already? Must be gunning for employee of the month."

"Your stuff sells itself."

"Come on in." Matt turned and held up one finger to the Buick parked down the street. Big Ed's eyes narrowed and he shot Matt a suspicious look. "You working with a partner now? That's not like you."

"No. Just getting a ride. Don't worry, she doesn't know anything."

"Better not." Big Ed closed the door and led Matt to the

living room. "Have a seat." Matt chose the couch and Big Ed settled into a leather recliner. "So you need another supply already? Those teens must have the reefer madness this month."

Matt shook his head. "No, I'm fine on weed. Most of the pills, too. I just need some more morphine."

"No shit?" Big Ed said. "That stuff is popular with your crowd, huh?"

Matt shrugged.

"That's weird," Big Ed said. "I don't hardly have anyone moving that stuff. I only keep a supply stream open for a couple of big-ticket customers." He tilted his head to regard Matt. "You must be getting a pretty good price out there."

"Decent."

The two were quiet. Big Ed rubbed a hand across his salt-and-pepper beard as he regarded Matt. He began the negotiation game.

"I'm afraid it's going to cost you more this time."

"Why's that?"

"Weed's steady, man. Steady as she goes. Easy to grow, cheap, reliable. I love that stuff."

Matt just looked at him.

"But pharmaceuticals, that's a different tale altogether. There's always some new federal regulation to worry about. And the people that hoard prescriptions, go to a bunch of different pharmacies, then resell? Most of them are flakes, man. No consistency."

Matt made a gesture with his hands: *Go on.*

"It's going to cost you double this time."

"Double?!"

Big Ed spread out his hands, palms up. "This is a business. I need to take market factors into consideration."

Matt's fingernails dug into his palms as his hands tightened into fists. He clenched his jaw and tried to keep his face neutral. "Double. There's no way."

Big Ed exhaled. He pursed his lips, and his gaze drifted to the ceiling as if the answer to this little dilemma was written there. "Actually . . . maybe there is a way. Something has come up. Maybe you could help me out and then I help you out?" When Matt didn't respond, he stood and poured himself a drink from the wet bar in the corner. He held up the bottle and a glass to Matt, an offer, but Matt shook his head. Big Ed sat back down with his drink. He sipped it a few times before saying anything.

"See, I have another job for you. A different job. Great money. You'll be able to buy all the morphine you want."

"What kind of job?"

"Transport. I have a load of product north of the border. Twenty pounds of X. I need it picked up and brought to a guy in the city. Only take you a few hours."

"I don't have a car."

"That can be arranged. The cost won't even come out of your cut. You'll make more money in three hours than you make in three months of selling."

Matt maintained his poker face. Dollar amounts swirled through his head along with visions of how much easier things would be. At least for a little while. Finally, with a force of will, he shook his head. "The border, that's federal."

"Only if you get popped." Big Ed shook his head dismissively. "You know how small the odds are on that? First time across, and no priors?" He smirked. "Besides, you're white, my man. No profiling to worry about. Hell, they'll wave you right through."

A car horn honked outside, maybe the Buick, but he didn't look to the window.

"Besides, you want to make money in this business, you're going to do some time sooner or later. Everybody does. Part of the game." Big Ed finished his drink and set the glass on an end table. "You can't let the possibility mess up your business decisions. I did a two-and-a-half-year stretch in my thirties. It's not as bad as they say. The food's terrible and it's boring as hell, but it's not a nightmare. It's not like the movies."

"Look, I hear you, all right?" Matt had a vision of himself sitting in a cage while Jack called out for him. The urge to pick up that empty glass and smash it in Big Ed's face was so strong that he barely trusted himself to move at all. He looked at the floor when he was able to speak. "I just can't afford to do any time right now."

Big Ed shook his head and sighed. "You need to start thinking about your future, you know? You only have—what?—a few more months in that school? Afterward you'll have very limited access to that market. It's time to start thinking about your niche after you get out."

Big Ed let the words hang there. The house suddenly felt more suffocating than the trailer.

"Seriously, I can't afford to do any time right now. Maybe in a few . . ." Matt stopped, something inside him unable to put a timetable on what would inevitably happen to Jack, even a vague one. "Maybe in a while I'll be able to risk it."

Big Ed stood, took his glass to the wet bar and washed it. When he spoke again he didn't look at Matt. "That's disappointing. But I'm glad you dropped by. We'll talk again when we have business to conduct together."

"And the morphine?"

"It's double."

Matt had to concentrate fiercely to keep himself under control. Now was not a good time to say—or do—something he would regret. He stood and walked to the door. "I'll see you later" was all he said.

THIRTEEN

When the trunk and the backseat of the Buick were filled with boxes of books, Amanda drove to the hospital and pulled into a visitors' parking space near the lobby.

"Thanks for all your help, Matt."

Matt checked the time on his phone. "Let's get these boxes into the lobby. I need to get going."

"Really? I was hoping there might be enough time to read a book to one of the kids. If someone's around, you know, if the time is right."

"I'll take the bus." Matt stepped onto the pavement, opened the back door and lifted a box.

"No, it's okay. I can swing by here tomorrow."

"Whatever."

Matt stacked another box on top of the one in his arms. As he did he heard sirens blare. He shrank against the car. An ambulance zoomed in and stopped abruptly at the nearby entrance to the emergency room.

The EMTs hopped out, opened the back doors and removed a gurney. An elderly man lay on the stretcher, an oxygen mask obscuring his face. One gnarled hand reached up, grasped at an EMT's sleeve, then slipped and fell back. As they rushed him past Matt and through the hospital doors the old man kept reaching up and grabbing, again and again, but never got a good grip.

"Fuck this," Matt said. He dropped the boxes on the curb and marched toward the parking lot exit.

He heard Amanda calling to him but he didn't slow down.

Matt missed the bus by two minutes and had to walk home. He kept checking the time on his phone, and when it hit four-thirty he ran the rest of the way.

Matt wrestled open the door of the trailer and scanned the front room. No mess in the kitchen. Blanket still folded on top of the couch. TV off.

His heart did a wavering thing, then redlined. He stalked down the hallway. "Jack?" Bedroom door closed. "Jack?" He pushed open the door. Jack lay still on the bed, eyes open, fixed on the ceiling. His face looked different, the cheeks a little more sunken, the lips looser somehow. Matt's breath came in fits and starts. "Jack?" He couldn't make his legs take the two steps to the bed. "Jack, I told you this wasn't funny anymore."

Jack was still for another moment before his head rolled on the pillow to face Matt. "No shit."

Matt felt his knees buckle with relief. He sat on the bed. "What are you doing?" Jack was quiet. "What are you still doing in here?"

"Playing tennis, kid, what's it look like?"

"Didn't you get out of bed today?"

Jack sighed. He shook his head but it barely moved. Matt reached to put his hand on the blanket covering Jack's leg, to make sure he was still there, but stopped before touching him. "Are you okay?"

"Stupid question."

"You know what I mean."

Jack coughed, short, staccato barks that grew louder and longer until it sounded like he was retching. He winced as his chest shuddered. Matt could only watch.

The coughing jag faded. Jack leaned over on one shoulder and reached for the tissues on the bedside table. His hand made a grasping motion although it was still a few feet away from the box. Matt pulled out a handful and held it up to Jack's face. Jack spat a brown glob into the wad of tissue. He fell back onto his pillow.

"I feel 'bout the same way I felt yesterday, if that's what yer askin'. And the day before that one."

"What have you had to eat today?"

Jack shook his head.

"Nothing? Why not?"

"Not hungry."

"Jesus, Jack." Matt stood up. His body wanted to pace, but there was no room. He tossed the tissue in the trash and took a deep breath. "Look, you have to take care of yourself. I'll make dinner. You want ice cream or the fish sticks?"

Jack made a face.

"Come on. What is this?" Matt moved closer to the bed and hovered over Jack, who turned his head the other way. "You're not giving up, are you?"

"Like it's my choice."

Matt stuffed his hands into his pockets so he wouldn't punch a hole through the faux-wood paneling. "What do you want? Huh? You wanna play cards? Watch TV? You want me to turn on the radio? There's gotta be something. You can't just lie in here. You can't."

Jack slowly raised one hand from underneath the blanket and scratched at his red-and-white beard. "You really wanna know what I want?"

"What?"

Jack turned his head to look at Matt again and smiled. For that moment he looked once again like the Jack that Matt remembered. "I wanna get laid. Just one more time before it's all over."

Matt grunted out what might have been a half-laugh and

shook his head. As he walked down the hall toward the kitchen area he called over his shoulder. "You bet, Jack. We'll hit the singles bars tonight. Right after dinner."

Matt's hands were shaking as he opened the refrigerator. He searched every shelf and drawer, desperately trying to find something—anything—that Jack would eat.

FOURTEEN

Matt sat at his usual table in the commons during break while people stopped by. A nervous first-timer who took five minutes to approach the table. An oblivious freshman handing out a survey for yearbook. A couple of girls who would do anything on a Saturday night in exchange for a party bag. None of them stayed long.

Matt was getting ready to leave when Amanda walked up. "Hey, Matt."

Matt raised his eyebrows in acknowledgment.

"I missed you at Helping Hands last week. I didn't do any pickups or anything. I just drew up some posters instead."

"Great."

Amanda shifted her bag from one hand to the other. "I just wanted to make sure that everything was okay?"

"Yep."

"That's good. I know that . . . well, sometimes hospitals freak me out, too. Especially the smell."

"Hospitals do not freak me out." Christ, why was she even talking about this?

"That's okay. I just . . . that's okay. So maybe I'll see you at the next meeting? I could still use some help and you're a lot better at carrying those boxes than me."

Before Matt could answer, a couple of guys, longtime customers, ambled up to the table. "What's up, bro?"

"Not much," Matt said.

The guys looked Amanda up and down, then glanced back at Matt. "You busy?"

"No."

"Can we talk business?"

Amanda cleared her throat. "Well, I have to get going, Matt. Maybe I'll see you next week. Bye."

"Whatever."

Amanda had just started walking away when one of the guys said, "What the hell?"

"Come on, Matt knows what's up," said the other guy. "It's obvious. Fat girls always give the best head. They love that stuff, right?" The first guy cracked up and offered a fist for bumping.

Matt watched Amanda's back, gauging the distance, trying to decide whether or not she had heard. "What do you guys want?"

■ ■ ■

Mr. Marsh sent Matt a note during Earth Science. When Matt showed up at his office, Marsh's desk was buried in paperwork.

"Sorry about the mess, Matt. Have a seat." Mr. Marsh shuffled a few papers around before giving up and tossing them on top of a pile. He sighed. "Progress reports go out this week. The athletes have to keep it above a 2.5 or they get kicked off teams. It's do-or-die time for a lot of seniors, so we have to notify parents. I'm swimming in it this week."

"But you still have time to pull me out of class."

"That's right." Mr. Marsh sat up straighter in his chair and smoothed his tie. "I guess you know why I called you in here today."

Matt tilted his head, waiting.

"The sign-up sheet to give a formal speech at the big Spring Varsity Week assembly goes up today. Auditions start in a few weeks. I knew you'd want to be first on the list." Mr. Marsh leaned forward, his serious eyes searching Matt's face for a few uncomfortable moments.

Matt couldn't remember selling Marsh any weed, but if he thought Matt was going to speak at an assembly then he was definitely on something.

Suddenly, Mr. Marsh threw his head back and laughed. Unrestrained belly laughs, too big for his little office. He clutched at the edge of his desk for support and knocked a stack of papers off, which made him laugh harder. Eventually, he collected himself. "I'm sorry, Matt. I'm teasing, of course. I just wanted to see the look on your face. And boy, you sure didn't disappoint." Mr. Marsh took off his glasses and wiped at his eyes. A couple of little hiccup-laughs bubbled up. "I needed that today. Thank you."

Matt just rolled his eyes and shook his head. "Good one, Mr. Marsh."

The counselor put his glasses back on and regarded Matt. "Man, you even get a sixty percent in Remedial Sense of Humor, don't you? Let's hope the school board doesn't start mandating field trips to the comedy clubs, trying to make sure you're a well-rounded citizen." Mr. Marsh sifted through piles of paper until he found the one he was looking for. "That reminds me of the first thing I wanted to talk to you about today. Seriously." He scanned the paper. "Ms. Edwards tells me you haven't been showing up to Helping Hands."

"Isn't she thorough."

"Give her a break, Matt. She notified me instead of Gill. Not everyone here is looking to jam you."

"I worked on one of their projects, this book drive thing. I'm good, right?"

"Can I bring you some news you should know already? Every meeting. I'll cut you a break. We'll forget the ones you missed, but you hit every meeting the rest of the school year. Starting now."

All traces of the smile were gone from Marsh's eyes. The two regarded each other in silence for a moment. "Come on, Matt, meet me halfway. Go to the meetings."

Matt stared straight ahead. "Fine."

Marsh rubbed his hands together like he was warming them up.

"Great. Now let me show you the second reason I called you in here today." He handed Matt a brochure. The glossy trifold had three circles on the cover. Each circle showed a group of multiethnic twentysomethings working on a task. Tinkering with a car engine, painting a house. "Tech's taking late applications this year."

"And?"

"And they require a diploma, two letters of recommendation, and a demonstration of skills in a particular program area."

"And?"

"Matt, I talked to every teacher you've had for high school science. They all said the same thing. You never once turned in a homework assignment and your participation in discussions was nonexistent, but they had to pass you because you aced all the in-class labs. Mr. Sixty Percent strikes again."

Matt flipped through the brochure and saw pictures of students laying the foundation for a house.

"I could write you one of the letters of recommendation. Mrs. Bishop, from physics, has agreed to write the other one. You know how she is—won't pretty up your attitude or anything, but she'll attest to your skills, and the fact that you show up every day. I think you've got a shot at getting in."

"More school." Matt closed the brochure. "You think that's what I'm after?"

"Flip it over to look at the back," Mr. Marsh said. Matt saw a picture of three students in safety goggles standing in front of a circuit board. "They have an electricians' program. There's a two-year apprenticeship, but you make money while you're doing it. Nothing special, but it's a decent living wage."

Matt skimmed the text, remembering Mrs. Bishop and her labs.

"Once you're done with the apprenticeship, you're a licensed electrician. And with the real estate market doing what it's doing around here, plus all the new buildings going up at the university, there's going to be more jobs than the local workforce can handle. That'll last for a while. As in quite a few years."

Matt studied the rest of the pictures on the brochure.

"By year four, you'd be making more money than I do. I'm not joking now," Mr. Marsh said. Matt looked up from the brochure and into Mr. Marsh's eyes. "By year seven, you'll make more than Mr. Gill."

Matt held up the brochure. "Can I keep this?"

"You bet," Mr. Marsh said. "Here, humor me, take an application, too." He handed Matt a manila folder full of papers. Matt stuck it under his arm.

Matt stood. "I better go back to class."

"All right, Matt, let me know if you want me to write that letter," Mr. Marsh said as Matt opened the door.

"If Ms. Edwards calls me again . . . ," Mr. Marsh added as Matt stepped into the hallway. Matt turned, his face carefully blank.

Mr. Marsh shrugged. "Just saying. If she does, I guess I'll know your answer."

FIFTEEN

Matt was already seated in 212, the room mostly full, when Amanda entered. She was wearing a brace that covered her palm and knuckles and extended to her elbow. She crossed to where Ms. Edwards was sitting at her desk, leaned over and whispered something in her ear, then chose a desk on the opposite side of the room.

Matt tried to keep himself from looking at the clock. He waited as long as he could stand, but each time he glanced at it the numbers had only changed by a minute or two. The papers on his desk shuffled and reshuffled themselves in his hands. He tried not to think about what might be happening at the trailer, but that was impossible.

He stood up and crossed the room. The other students were

sitting in circles, absorbed in their discussions. Matt walked to Amanda's desk.

"Hey."

Amanda looked up.

"You still doin' the book drive?"

Amanda showed off her arm brace. "It was hard enough before. Now it's pretty much impossible."

"Sorry." Matt shuffled his feet. He jerked his head in the direction of his desk and all those papers. "Edwards said she'd give me credit if I came in and did stuff for her. TA-type stuff. Today's alphabetizing."

Amanda just looked at him.

Matt cleared his throat. "But I'd, uh, rather be out in the car, you know? Than in here. Being in this building after last period is brutal."

Amanda's forehead creased. "Matt, if that's an invitation, it's the worst one I've had all year."

"Whatever." Matt turned to walk back to his desk.

"Wait," Amanda said. She pushed herself out of her chair using her good arm. "Unfortunately, it's the *only* one I've gotten this year. Let's go pick up some books."

Matt checked out with Ms. Edwards and followed Amanda through the door.

They were mostly quiet as the Buick drove through the rain. The windshield wiper on Matt's side was old and useless; it blurred the words on street signs and smeared the headlights of other cars across the glass. He pulled his denim jacket tighter around his shoulders.

"Sorry about the heater. It only works in the summer." Amanda gave him a pale smile.

"No problem."

They stopped for pickups, one after another. Each time after Matt set the box between them, Amanda would look through the books before driving away. "So many good ones," she said. She held up an old copy of *Are You My Mother?* "This one used to make me want to cry." She pulled out *Fox in Socks*. "My mom and I used to see who could read this one the fastest. I think she let me win." Amanda looked at Matt. "What were some of your favorites? Growing up?"

Matt studied the dashboard. "Not a big reader."

Amanda pulled back into traffic, sloshing through puddles. The Buick was at a stoplight when Matt's phone rang.

He checked the number. The trailer. His stomach went cold. He glanced at Amanda, then answered the call.

"Hey. Everything okay?" Matt spoke in hushed tones.

"Yeah, yeah, everything's fine." The raspy voice was unmistakably Jack's.

"What do you need?"

"Huh? Talk louder. Can't hardly hear you."

"What do you want?"

"I need you to pick something up for me."

Matt couldn't remember the last time Jack had asked for something from town. "What?"

"Halloween cards."

"Hallo . . ." Matt glanced at Amanda. She kept her eyes carefully focused on the road. He shifted in his seat so that he was facing the side window. "Hallo*ween* cards?" he whispered. "I told you to only use this number for an emergency."

"Yeah. Halloween cards. A big box of 'em. I need lots."

Matt shook his head, the hand not holding the phone clenched into a fist. "Do you know what month it is?"

"Huh? What are you, talking with a sock in your mouth?"

"Do you have any idea how long it is until Halloween?"

"Course I do. I'm not that far gone, you little shit."

"It's not that." Matt tried to keep his voice low. "I just . . . Don't you get it? No place will be selling those right now."

"Just bring me a bunch a them cards." The line went dead.

Matt took great care in putting his phone back in his pocket, the overly calm gesture a substitute for smashing it against the dashboard.

The Buick slipped under a freeway overpass, the steady pounding of the rain disappearing for a moment before starting up again.

After a few minutes Amanda softly said, "Matt?" He was staring out the window. "Matt?"

"Huh?"

"I don't want you to think I was eavesdropping. You know, not on purpose or anything. But I think I know a place."

"What kind of place?"

"That sells Halloween cards. Even now."

Matt looked over at her. "Yeah?"

"The Dollars Discount store, behind the old business district downtown. They have a seasonal section with all the holidays."

"I think I know that place."

"My mom and I go there sometimes." Amanda giggled. "They sell those marshmallow Peeps in the Easter section. Sometimes we buy a few packages before we go out to the movies."

"They keep that stuff in stock?"

"Probably not. I think it's just stuff left over from the last year." Amanda's cheeks went pink. "But come on, they're *Peeps*. Those things have enough preservatives to survive a nuclear winter."

"Mmmmm," Matt said. "Year-old candy. Tasty."

"Are you making fun of me?"

Matt shook his head. "Not really. I used to like those, too." It was quiet for a few moments. "Sorry to be a pain in the ass, but do you mind if we swing by there before we pick up the next box of books?"

SIXTEEN

Matt walked a crooked line down the deeply pitted gravel road between the trailers, dodging puddles. He had told Amanda to drop him off up at the main road before the entrance to the park. The rain had slowed to a drizzle and the picnic table regulars were back out, huddled inside frayed Goodwill Windbreakers, lighting cigarettes underneath cupped palms.

"Look at that. He's more reliable'n the goddamn United States Postal Service."

"Hell, yes. Not wind or rain or any of that shit gonna slow that boy down."

"You got any deliveries for us, today? Maybe a little discount for your Meadow Street Estates brothers?"

Matt gave a small wave and entered trailer #6. He took off

his jacket and shook it over the square of carpet they used for a mat before draping it over a kitchen chair.

Jack sat in the recliner, wrapped up in a blanket. A fuzzy game show played soundlessly on the TV. "'Bout time. What took you so long?"

"Nothing. I had some stuff to do."

"Did you bring 'em?"

"Bring what?"

"The Halloween cards. What's wrong with you?"

"Oh, shit." Matt threw up his hands in frustration. "I must've left 'em in her trunk. I'll get 'em tomorrow, okay?"

Jack sat up straighter in the recliner. *"Her?"* he said. "You holdin' out on me?"

"Never mind."

"You got a girlfriend and you don't bring her by here?"

"It's not like that."

Jack snorted. "Like hell it ain't like that. I was a teenager, you know. It's always like that." He shook his head. "I can't believe you have a 'her' and you never told me about it."

"It's not like that."

"Is she real pretty?"

"No."

"No matter. A girl that's too pretty is usually a big pain in your ass."

"You're a big pain in my ass."

Jack chuckled and wheezed, grabbing a pack of cigarettes from the coffee table. Matt walked around the trailer, picking up random pieces of clothing and dumping the ashtray gunk into the trash.

"We're almost outta them morphine pills," Jack said.

"I know."

"I'm gonna need some more soon. Real soon."

Matt sighed. "I'll take care of it."

He continued to clean up. There was an uproar outside and Matt peered through the tiny kitchen window. The Buick Electra sat in the middle of the gravel road, Amanda talking to the guys assembled there. The picnic table regulars were laughing, shouting over each other. A couple of them pointed to trailer #6.

Matt jumped out the front door as the Buick pulled up in front of the trailer. "What are you doing here?"

"You forgot to take your cards. I thought I'd—"

"Right. Just pop the trunk and I'll get 'em." Matt rushed to the rear of the Buick, ignoring the catcalls from the men on the picnic tables.

Amanda opened the door and pushed herself onto the gravel. "I can't pop it open, the knob thingy is broken. You have to use the keys." She walked to the rear of the car.

Matt glanced at the door of the trailer. "Okay, just hurry."

Amanda had to jiggle the key before the latch clicked open. "I think we'll be able to get them out in time, Matt. It won't be Halloween for quite a few months."

Matt pushed open the trunk and picked up the box of cards. "Thanks. I'll see you at school, okay? Bye." He turned toward the trailer.

"Hello, young missy!" Jack leaned against the doorframe in his bathrobe.

"Oh, shit," Matt muttered.

"Hi!" Amanda called, waving. "I was just dropping some stuff off for Matt."

"We appreciate it. Why don't you come in and say hello?"

"You don't want to do that," Matt said. "I'll see you at—"

"Sure," Amanda said, pushing past Matt. She walked to the front door and held her hand out to Jack. "I'm Amanda."

"A pleasure. We don't get none too many visitors around here. 'Specially not ladies." Jack took Amanda's hand in his. He leaned forward slowly, carefully, bracing himself against the doorframe with his free arm, and kissed Amanda's hand.

"Aren't you sweet?" Amanda said.

"One of us has gotta be. If you been with Matt I'm sure ya noticed he's not exactly schooled in the social graces. I blame his mother for that." Jack's eyes crinkled up as he chuckled.

"Tell me about it." Amanda joined Jack in his laughter. "No chance you two are related, then?"

"I'm his uncle, but don't hold that against me, young lady." They both laughed some more. "Come on in, if you got a free minute. We can get a pot of coffee going. Matt buys terrible stuff but at least he gets a lot of it."

Amanda turned her head and looked back at Matt. He shook his head, his mouth in a straight line. Amanda flashed him a smile. "A cup of coffee sounds great." She followed Jack, squeezing through the door and into the kitchen area.

Matt stared at the trailer. "Shit."

SEVENTEEN

The three of them sat at the kitchen table, hands wrapped around chipped coffee mugs for the warmth. Jack and Amanda talked and laughed while Matt mostly stared at the table.

"So how'd you come to have that brace on your arm?" Jack said.

"Oh, it's embarrassing," Amanda said. "I was helping my mom carry groceries into the house and I slipped in our driveway. I sat there in a puddle of broken eggs and spilt milk, crying my eyes out." She held up her brace for them to see. "I dislocated the wrist and fractured my forearm bone."

"Ouch!"

"I'll say. I have to wear this thing for the next two months." Amanda regarded the brace, then gestured toward her body with her good arm. "I guess this is an awful lot of weight to be crashing down on top of an arm."

"Now don't you worry yourself about that none. There ain't nothing wrong with bein' a big girl. Nothing at all."

"Jack, please," Matt said.

"What? It's true."

"Who cares? You don't have to talk about it."

"Why not? I've been lucky enough to be with more'n a few big women in my life. Some a my best memories, if you want to know the truth."

"Jesus, Jack! Don't be disgusting."

"What's disgusting? Big women ain't disgusting."

"You know I didn't mean that." Matt glanced at Amanda. "I didn't mean that at all."

Matt and Jack stared at each other. A car splashed by outside the trailer. Amanda cleared her throat. "It's okay, Matt, really," she said. She put her hand on Matt's arm briefly. "Most people just pretend not to notice that part of me. And then they end up not seeing me at all, you know? It's okay to talk about stuff." Her cheeks went pink. "Even if it is a little . . . forward."

"Amen. Better'n bein' backward." Jack smirked at Matt. Matt glared in return.

"Let me get you a refill on that coffee," Jack said. He tried to push himself out of his chair but his arm slipped and he fell back. Matt reached out reflexively to catch him, steady him, but Jack pushed his arm away. He started coughing then and it degenerated into one of his hacking jags; he held himself steady on the table, head bent over until the fit passed. When it was done he looked a little embarrassed. The silence in the trailer sat heavily for a few moments.

"Hey, is that a cribbage board?" Amanda said, looking at one of the shelves. "I love cribbage."

"You do?" Jack said.

"My mom taught me how in elementary school when I was having trouble in math. We play all the time."

"There's hope for the younger generation yet," Jack said. "You wanna play? I get tired of whipping up on Matt here, and we ain't played a game of three-way since . . . well, it's been a long time, hasn't it, Matt?"

"Four years and three months," Matt said.

"Sounds like it's 'bout time to try it again."

"Amanda probably needs to go."

"It's okay. My mom's working late tonight, so I'm on my own. Deal me in."

Matt sighed, pulled the board down from the shelf and slowly shuffled the cards.

An hour later Amanda's cribbage peg rounded the final corner on the game board. She was nearing her third straight blowout victory when Jack winced and clutched at his belly. "Oof."

"You okay?" Matt said.

"I think so, it's just . . ." Jack tried to use the table as leverage to stand up, but he fell to one knee on the kitchen linoleum.

Matt jumped out of his seat and grabbed Jack around the

shoulders. He glanced quickly at Amanda before returning his attention to Jack. "Do you need to get to the bathroom?" he whispered. He pulled Jack into a half-standing position.

"No, I need—" Jack gasped in pain and his knees buckled. Matt clutched him with both hands, braced himself and took on Jack's full weight. "Chair," Jack wheezed, clutching at his belly with both hands.

"How can I help?" Amanda said, getting out of her chair.

Matt stumbled with Jack to the recliner and let him slump over on top of it. Jack's eyes were wide, beads of sweat popping up on his forehead. His bathrobe fell open and he clawed at his belly. "Hurts." Matt could barely hear the word. He glanced at the clock.

"Did you take your morphine on time?"

Jack's breath was ragged. "Think . . . so."

Matt marched to the bathroom. He opened the medicine cabinet and scanned the messy shelves. He found the morphine container, popped it open and spilled a few pills onto his hand. They were white, not blue. Aspirin. "Shit." He opened the aspirin bottle, saw that it was filled with an assortment of pills, muscle relaxants and cold and flu gelcaps. Jack had been messing with the meds again. Matt shook out all the pills inside the morphine canister, but it was all aspirin. Jack must've taken it by mistake.

Matt left the bathroom and opened the hall closet. He pulled a jar from the pocket of a winter coat, unscrewed the lid and fished out a wad of bills. When he counted the amount that Big Ed needed, the jar was almost empty. A feeling of total despair hit Matt so hard it felt like he was going to fall down. He clung to the handle on the closet door for support and closed his eyes.

It took him a few moments to collect himself and put the jar back into the coat. He shoved the money into the pocket of his jeans.

He rushed to the living room. Jack was moaning, his eyes closed and his face twisted into a grimace. Amanda knelt beside him. She held one of his hands with the fingers sticking out of her brace, and with her good hand she dabbed at his forehead with a wet paper towel.

"I need to run and get him something."

"My keys are on the table. Take my car."

"Are you sure?"

Amanda nodded. Jack cried out so loudly that she flinched.

"Do you mind staying with him while I'm gone?"

"No."

"I'm really sorry, but—"

"Just hurry."

Matt bolted through the doorway of the trailer.

EIGHTEEN

Matt drummed his fingers nervously on the steering wheel of the Buick, waiting to merge with the after-work traffic snaking past the entrance to the trailer park on the main road. He'd finally spotted a small opening behind an approaching pickup truck when Janice banged open the door of her manager's trailer and stalked toward the car.

When she got close she made the roll-your-window-down gesture. Matt fumbled with the controls until he found the right one.

Janice planted her feet in front of the driver's-side door, smacking her gum and holding a cigarette. "What the hell is this, kid?"

"What do you mean?"

"You got money for a car now but not the rent?"

"What?"

"Rent was due Friday. *Last* Friday. Now you're driving around in this?" Janice waved her cigarette up and down the length of the Buick.

"Shit." Matt smacked his palm on top of the steering wheel. "I forgot, really. Things have been . . . it's been crazy, you know?"

"Things are crazy for everyone, kid. Always. You wouldn't believe the stuff I hear when the first a the month rolls around. I still need that money."

"This isn't even my car. I swear."

"Doesn't matter. I was gonna stop by your place today anyway. You got the rent or not?"

The feeling hit Matt again, like there was a weight on top of his chest and it just kept pressing down, getting heavier and heavier. It took a physical effort to get breath into his body, to squeeze the air past that invisible weight and into his lungs. He got that feeling almost every day lately.

Janice stopped her smacking long enough to blow a long stream of smoke. "Look, don't make me go through the same threats I have to use with some a these clowns." She jerked her head in the direction of a row of trailers. "You're a smart kid, you know what happens if I don't get that money. Right?"

The air leaked from Matt in a long sigh, leaving him feeling deflated. He dug into his pocket and pulled out the stack of bills. After he counted what he owed Janice there wasn't much left.

"Thanks, kid. Take it easy." Janice turned and walked back to her trailer.

Matt stared at the few remaining bills in his palm.

The familiar noises of the trailer park pulled him out of it. Slamming doors, barking dogs. He glanced in the rearview mirror at trailer #6, then pushed the nose of the Buick toward the traffic on the main road, trying to find a way in.

NINETEEN

It took Big Ed an eternity to answer the doorbell. Matt stood on the front porch, waiting for the invitation to step inside. None was offered.

"Hey," he said.

"What do you need?"

"The morphine."

Big Ed grunted. "You have the money, then? The price we agreed on?"

"Not all of it." Matt cleared his throat. "But I can pay you back. With interest."

Big Ed slowly folded his arms across his chest and remained silent. Matt spoke to the welcome mat, unable to look the man in the eyes. The words came out too quickly, no confidence behind them. "I have it all figured so it works for both of us—

fifty percent of my profits for the next two months. That should make it worth your while." Matt hated the desperation in his own voice. "You know I'm good for it."

Big Ed shook his head. "Business doesn't work that way, Matt. At least not a good business. You know this."

Matt clenched his fingers into fists, grinding his teeth together and willing himself to make the necessary mental shift. The words stuck in his throat.

Big Ed placed one hand on the doorknob and started to ease the door shut. "If that's all, then I'll see you in a couple of weeks. For your normal appointment."

"Wait," Matt said. He put one palm flat on the door. He could feel the seconds, minutes, rushing past.

"Yes?"

Matt spoke in a low voice, through clenched teeth. "Is that transport job still available?"

Big Ed smiled. "That's better." He pushed the door wide open. "There's always a transport job available." He swept his hand toward the living room. "Come on in, I'll give you all the details. And we'll get that morphine for you."

Matt lowered his head and walked through the door.

TWENTY

It took a concentrated effort to hold the Buick to the speed limit on the way home. When Matt finally arrived at the trailer, he raced to yank open the door.

Amanda was sitting on the kitchen floor, her back against the fridge. Jack lay sprawled on his side on the linoleum, his head in Amanda's lap, his eyes closed. She was stroking his head and whispering softly.

"Jesus," Matt whispered. He knelt down and almost touched Jack. "Is he . . . you know, okay?" Matt couldn't make himself say the word *alive*.

Amanda nodded. Her face had gone white, her eyes red. "He finally passed out. From the pain," she whispered.

The tension drained from Matt and he slumped backward, sitting on the floor beside them. He looked around the kitchen area. The chairs from the little table were overturned, lying on their sides. Dirty dishes were scattered across the floor near the sink, some of them broken in half. "Are *you* okay?"

Amanda tried to smile but her lips trembled. When she blinked, tears slipped from the corners of her eyes and ran down her cheeks. "It was . . ." She paused and took a few shaky breaths. "It got pretty bad there for a little while. But I'm okay."

Matt stared at Jack, trying to take some comfort in the slight rise and fall of his chest. "I know how he gets when the pain is really bad. It's scary." He remembered Jack's first big pain fit. Matt hadn't been that terrified since he was a little kid hiding in his bedroom and praying for the bad noises from the living room to stop.

He took a deep breath. "I'm sorry you had to go through that. It's my fault."

Amanda shook her head, wiping the tears away with the back of her hand. "It's okay. I was scared for him, not me." Her other hand was still steadily smoothing down what was left of Jack's hair. "Were you able to make it to the pharmacy?"

"Huh? Oh, yeah, I have some stuff right here." Matt pulled a plastic Baggie of pills out of his pocket. Amanda studied the Baggie but didn't say anything. "We'll have to sit him up so he can take these." Matt bent over and slipped an arm between Amanda's legs and Jack's shoulder. Amanda twisted to give him room, then wrapped her good arm around Jack's middle to help Matt pull. Jack moaned horribly, his head twisting back and forth.

"Careful," Matt said. "That's where he hurts the most."

Amanda shifted her grip to Jack's upper chest. Together they pulled him until he was sitting upright against the fridge.

"He's so light," Amanda said.

"I know," Matt said. He patted Jack on the cheek. "Hey, Jack," he whispered. "Can you wake up for me? I have some pills for you." Jack gasped and moaned, his eyes still closed. One hand reached up and made a halfhearted attempt to push Matt away. "Come on, Jack. This is the good stuff."

Jack's eyes opened to half-mast, cloudy and unfocused. When the light hit them, he sucked in air and clutched his belly with both hands. "Hurts," he wheezed, his face contorted into a grimace. "Christ, it hurts so bad."

"I know, Jack. I'm sorry."

"You can understand what he's saying?" Amanda said.

"Yeah. You, uh, get used to it, you know?" Matt cupped one of Jack's hands in his own and placed three morphine tablets in the palm. "Let's take these, okay? You'll feel better. I promise." Matt's voice was as soothing as he could make it.

Jack's fingers were gnarled into odd shapes and his hand shook. He stared over Matt's shoulder. Matt tried to help him raise his hand to his mouth but the pills slipped out of Jack's hand and scattered across the linoleum. Jack didn't even notice. Matt picked them up off the floor and tried again. Same result.

"Shit," Matt muttered. "Here, hold him for a second." Amanda kept Jack propped up while Matt stood and rummaged through the kitchen cabinets. He found a shot glass, dumped the pills into it and then added a little water from the tap.

Matt knelt down again beside Jack and Amanda. He held the back of Jack's neck and tilted his head backward. Amanda helped him keep Jack's head steady and he poured in the contents of the shot glass. Jack's head jerked in surprise and he sputtered, but Matt and Amanda kept him propped up until he choked down the pills and water.

They held him together on the kitchen floor until his moaning got quieter and slower. It was impossible to tell how long they sat there, but it was long enough for Matt's knees and back to stiffen painfully in his awkward position on the floor. Finally, Jack's moaning softened and faded until it became light snoring.

When Jack's hands fell away from where they had been clutching at his belly, Matt exhaled heavily and slumped against a kitchen cabinet.

After staring at the ceiling for a while, breathing deeply, he looked at Amanda. Her eyes were still red but otherwise she looked like she was okay. "I don't know what to say."

"You don't have to say anything, Matt."

He leaned his head back until it rested against the cabinet. They were quiet for several minutes. The sounds of the trailer park filtered through the thin walls, but the only thing Matt had ears for was the sound of Jack continuing to draw air into his lungs.

"You know what?" Matt said.

"What?"

"If you don't make it into that nursing school I'm going down to the admissions office to beat the shit out of somebody."

Amanda laughed. The sound filled up the tiny room. She stopped abruptly, her cheeks tinged with pink. "Thank you, Matt. That's very sweet," she said. "I think."

Matt sighed and stood up. "I need to get him into bed. Hopefully he can rest until morning."

Matt bent down, put one arm behind Jack's head and the other behind his knees, then picked him up, like he was a little kid. He carried Jack sideways down the narrow hallway and placed him in bed.

TWENTY-ONE

When Matt returned to the living room the kitchen chairs were upright again and Amanda was picking broken bits of plate off the floor.

"You don't have to do that. I can—"

"Shhhhh. You'll wake him up."

Matt put on a new pot of coffee. They cleaned together in silence, Amanda doing the dishes while Matt swept up the last of the broken plates. When they were finished they sat at the table together with fresh cups.

"I'm sorry you had to—"

"Matt, stop apologizing, okay? I'm glad I could help. Really."

Matt allowed his muscles to unclench a little and he settled into his chair. They sipped at their coffee.

"Have you been managing all this . . . alone?" Amanda's voice was just a whisper.

Matt was silent, his stare threatening to burn a hole in the table.

"I'm sorry," she said. "It's none of my business. I'll just—"

Matt held up a hand, cutting her off.

"Yes," he said. "I've been doing it alone. Managing." He exhaled slowly. "Barely."

Amanda reached out and briefly patted Matt's forearm as it rested on the table.

"Jack seems like a great guy."

Matt nodded.

"I guess he must be pretty sick?"

"Yeah." Matt studied his hands. "Yeah, he has . . ." Matt stopped. Neither he nor Jack had ever said the word out loud, not even to each other.

Matt felt like needles were poking at the insides of his eyeballs, making them burn. He stared straight ahead, trying not to think about anything and not to blink. Blinking when your eyes are all hot like that means tears will come out, even if you don't mean for them to.

"Are you okay?"

Matt nodded. More silence.

"When I was five years old my dad died," Amanda said. "I thought I'd never get over it. Sometimes I still think I'll never get over it. Not really."

Matt chewed on his lip.

"He had a heart attack. I remember being really mad at his

doctor. I know it sounds silly but I was mad at his doctor for a lot of years."

Matt thought back to the calm face of Jack's doctor. Too calm. Matt had felt like pounding the guy just to get that look off his face.

"That doesn't sound silly," Matt said.

They sipped at their coffee for a few more minutes. "How long has he been sick?"

"We don't know. Probably a long time. But we found out about a year ago."

Matt remembered the day too well. Coming home from school, surprised to find Jack's car parked outside already. When he went inside he heard the strangest sounds. He had found Jack in the bathroom, sitting on the toilet with his pants around his ankles. Jack was slumped over, clutching at the shower curtain for support, some of the rings hanging empty from where he had ripped the curtain away.

Matt didn't know at what point in the recollection he had started talking. But it felt like a plug had been pulled and all the words were draining out of him.

"He couldn't take a shit, said it had been over a week. I guess he'd been chomping on Ex-Lax for a few days by that point. I'd seen him mad before, real mad sometimes, and I'd heard him yell and scream, but I'd never seen anything like that. He sounded like he didn't have any control over himself. Like a wounded animal. Scared the shit outta me."

Saying the words to another actual person for the first time intensified the memory. Jack shaking all over, his hands trembling and his whole body rocking with convulsions. His forehead and shirt drenched in sweat.

Matt had retreated to the living room of the trailer, scared, but at first more embarrassed to have seen Jack like that. When the growling and screaming didn't stop, he eventually crept back down the hall.

"I managed to get him out of there. Laid him down in the backseat and drove his car to the emergency room. They said he had 'intestinal blockage' and needed surgery right away. I sat in the lobby all night.

"When I got in to see him the next day he looked like a ghost. Worse. The skeleton of a ghost. He didn't want to talk about it. Maybe didn't want me to know right away."

The picture on the hospital room TV had been fuzzy, the sound too low to hear much of the dialogue or canned laughter of some mindless sitcom. But he and Jack had watched for hours, Matt sitting on a hard plastic chair pulled up next to Jack's bed.

Matt sipped his coffee for a while before continuing. "I finally got it out of him. He told me that when the doctors cut open his stomach to remove the blockage, they found the . . . you know." Matt tried to fight off that burning needle feeling behind his eyes again. "They found the cancer."

There it was, finally, the word raw and blood-flecked, forced from his throat.

"I guess it was . . . all over the place inside him, you know? Just everywhere they looked. We never had any health insurance or anything, so he hadn't been to see any doctors in a lot of years. When I look back now I think we both knew something was wrong. Had known for a while, probably. He'd been losing energy, doing less, sleeping more. For a few years, probably, but it was slow. You know, real gradual. I don't know what he was thinking about it because we never talked about stuff like that, but I think I just told myself it was because he was getting older, even though he's not really that old. Not near as old as he looks now."

Sometimes Matt wondered whether he'd even be able to recognize Jack if he hadn't been with him through the sickness. If Jack had left for a year and then come back the way he was now, Matt didn't think he'd be able to make the connection to the Jack he grew up with. Even now, it was hard sometimes. The cancer had eaten away so much of that person he used to know.

"Did the surgery help at all?" Amanda said. Matt blinked, Amanda's question bringing him back to the little kitchen area in the trailer.

"They were able to clear out the blockage—he eventually got to take his shit—but beyond that there was nothing they could do.

"He had to stay in the hospital for a week and he let me sit in the room when the doctors came to talk to him. There were a lot of them, and they all said a bunch of different things. But the only thing I heard then, and the only thing I remember now, is two words: *pain management.*

"It meant there was nothing they could do. Or maybe

nothing they would do. No chemo, no more surgeries, no experimental drugs. Nothing. Just pain management. Just try to keep him comfortable until . . . you know, until it's all over."

Matt held out his hands, palms up. "So that's what I've been doing. But I don't always do the best job, as you can obviously see."

Amanda dabbed at the corners of her eyes with the end of her sleeve. "I'm so sorry," she said. "I know that's a lame thing to say in situations like this, but I'm sorry." Matt pressed his lips together and nodded. "Have you tried to get any help? I know they have outpatient nursing programs, or you could call hospice. It must be so hard to be trying to do all of this all by yourself."

Matt shook his head. "That's the other part. I'm not even supposed to be living with him. You know, legally." He stopped and looked around the room as if just realizing where he was. "I shouldn't even be talking about this." He stood and dumped the rest of his coffee, then stared out the window above the sink.

Amanda got up from her chair and brought her cup over to Matt. He poured it down the drain, never taking his eyes from the window.

"If you need all this to stay quiet, you know the best part about sharing it with me?"

"What's that?"

"I have, like, three total followers on all of my social media accounts. Combined. And one of those is my mom." She sighed heavily, for effect. "And . . . okay, so another one is a fake account I made for my cat."

Matt grunted something that might have been a laugh.

"Sorry. Lame joke." Amanda briefly placed her hand on Matt's shoulder. "I'm just trying to tell you that your secret is safe with me. You know, if you want to talk." Matt continued to stare out the window until Amanda took a step away. "But you don't have to tell me," she hurriedly added. "I can leave and let you get some rest. If you ever do want to talk, though, I just want you to know that you can trust me."

Matt turned his head and looked at her. Really looked at her. He believed her. And he didn't want her to leave. He wasn't ready for the silence of the trailer just yet.

"Can I ask you a question?"

"Of course."

Matt crossed his arms over his chest and stared at her. "Can your cat keep his damn mouth shut?"

"Matt! Was that actually a joke?"

He grunted again. "Come here," he said.

She followed him into the living room area and took a seat on the couch while he perched on the arm of Jack's recliner. "My living situation has been messed up for kind of a long time." He studied his hands for a while before starting again.

"I never met my dad," he said. "My mom had to leave when I was thirteen. I lived on my own for a couple of months until CPS caught up with me. I think someone at school must have tipped them off.

"They gave me two choices. Live with my grandma or go into foster care. I had only seen my grandma a couple times, but it was enough to know that I didn't want to live there. And I don't know if you know much about foster care, but I had a couple buddies in middle school that were in the system. Sounded like it really sucked."

Matt's stomach went cold at the memory of that time. Life with his mother had been full of times that were difficult and often frightening, but at least he had come to know what to expect. The uncertainty and loneliness of the alone months had been much worse.

"That's when Jack came back. He was always traveling, bouncing around from one job to the next, but he would always come and crash with us for a few weeks, or a few months, in between. Those times were the best. And even when he wasn't there, he never forgot a birthday or Christmas. Even Halloween. Only mail I've ever gotten in my life was from him."

Matt paused and shook his head. What the hell would next Christmas be like?

It was quiet for a while. Eventually, Amanda said, "He came back for good that time?"

"Yeah, when Jack found out what was going on, he decided to stay with me until I got through high school. It might not sound like much, but for a guy like that, always on the go, to stay in one spot is a pretty big deal.

"But he knew he couldn't make it official, you know, fill out the paperwork and be an official foster care guy or whatever. He'd done some time here and there and probably had a few warrants out for all I know. So we never told anybody. If there's ever any forms that we can't get around filling out, from school or wherever, we list my bio-dad's mom's address as mine. She's never been in the picture, but at least it keeps anyone from any agency from sniffing around. But we can't go signing up for any social services or anything. People start asking questions, and we can't afford that. Can't afford for them to try and make me live someplace else. With someone else."

Amanda offered a comforting pat on his arm but remained silent.

"We get along together, you know? And it was fine, and would still be fine, if he hadn't gotten sick. We've been fine. It's always been just the two of us."

Matt didn't notice the pain in his throat until he tried to swallow and it felt like a golf ball was lodged in there. "But pretty soon it's only gonna be one of us."

TWENTY-TWO

Saying it out loud had made it more real. Matt was going to be alone.

Back at school it became difficult, for the first time, to maintain his 60 percent average. While his teachers droned on he found himself picturing it, aloneness, maybe trying to prepare himself for what lay ahead. But for some reason it was impossible to imagine. He could picture an empty trailer. He could picture Jack not being there. There had been lots of times when Jack had not been there while he was growing up, for a few weeks or even several months. What he could not imagine was Jack not coming back. The rational side of him knew it was going to happen, but the other part of him didn't know what that could possibly feel like.

Amanda stopped by the trailer the next day with a magazine

for Jack and a plate of food for Matt. But Matt didn't feel like talking anymore. Didn't feel like he could. Jack was taking a nap, and Matt just turned out all the lights and drew the curtains. After knocking a few times, Amanda left her gifts on the makeshift wooden steps outside the front door.

He avoided her the next week at school, too. Matt thought that might help him deal, not talking to anyone about this again. Maybe allow him to block everything out of his mind.

It didn't.

With a few minutes left in the lunch period, Matt was still talking to a group of guys in the stairwell by the gym. The junior prom was coming up and everyone wanted to make sure they had enough weed and pills for their parties. Usually Matt had a more take-it-or-leave-it stance on how much he could offer—he didn't want to have to listen to everyone's stories and try to adjust his amounts with Big Ed—but he could use the extra money this month. He checked the time and made an excuse to get away from those guys. He walked to the lunchroom.

On the way, he had extra sensors out for Gill and Hershey. Those two had been entirely too quiet lately, and no way did Matt believe it had anything to do with his attendance at Helping Hands. Getting frisked on a weekly basis might've been a pain in the ass, but it was better than wondering what they were up to.

When he got to the cafeteria, Amanda was sitting at one of the smaller tables, homework spread over the table and her backpack on an empty chair.

"Hey."

"Hi, Matt."

"So . . . how's it goin'?"

She gave him a half-smile. "Not bad. Just trying to catch up on some science homework."

"Right." Matt looked around the cafeteria. Pulled out a chair halfway but didn't sit down. Pushed it back.

He didn't know how to say what he came to say. Or even if he should say it. The only person he had ever asked anything from was Jack.

Amanda broke the awkward silence. "Actually, if I'm being honest, the homework is just a distraction."

"Yeah?"

"Yeah. I had this interview. For nursing school. It wasn't . . . I don't think it went very well."

"What? Come on. You're good at talking. Who wouldn't like you, if they sit down and talk to you for an hour?"

Amanda's smile was the biggest he'd ever seen on her, but she looked away and shook her head. "I wish. I started . . . it's so embarrassing."

"What?" Matt pulled the seat halfway out again.

Amanda took a deep breath. "I started crying. Not, like, bad-crying, you know? But they were asking about my experience with sick people, and I started to think about that little bit of time I got to spend with Jack." Her eyes filled with tears, but she continued. "I just . . . it really hit me. The people I would be working with—they are real people with real families who care about them. Like Jack." She paused. "Like my dad."

Matt sat down.

"Anyway, I don't know when I'll hear back, but I think I blew it. They probably think I'm a basket case." Amanda gestured to the papers on the table. "So I think I'm just trying to take my mind off it."

"I know what you mean." They were quiet for a moment.

Amanda wiped her eyes and sat up a bit straighter. "Oh, I can't believe I'm making this about me. How's Jack feeling? I should have asked right away."

It took Matt a while to get started.

"He's . . . I don't know. I guess the pain is mostly under control, but he's been sleeping a ton this week. And he doesn't eat very much. I mean, he hasn't eaten much for a long time, but I think it's getting worse."

"I'm so sorry to hear that," Amanda said. She looked down. "After stopping by your place a few times . . . I just . . . I mean, I've been trying to give you a little space now, you know? But if you need anything I hope you know I'm here."

Matt nodded. He got out of his chair and turned to go, then looked back at Amanda. "Look . . . Jack's been asking about you."

"Yeah?" she said. Her eyes brightened. "I've been thinking about him a lot. Not just when I'm crying in interviews." She smiled. "I've been thinking about both of you, actually. Hope you're doing okay."

They looked at each other in silence. The words Matt had found in the trailer were more elusive here in the school commons with the drone of a dozen meaningless conversations all around them.

"I've been wanting to do something special for him," Amanda said. "I don't know, something girly. Knit him a blanket or something. I know that must sound stupid."

Matt shook his head.

"I don't even know how to knit," she said.

Matt almost smiled. "Okay, maybe that does sound a little stupid, then."

Amanda smiled big enough for both of them. "I told you," she said. "Anyway, please tell him I said hello, okay? I hope he's feeling better. As well as he can, anyway. You know what I mean."

"Okay, I will, and, uh . . ." When the right words finally came, they came in a rush. He couldn't believe he was actually going to ask her for this, but what was the alternative? "Okay, so it's fine if you say no, really, but there's this errand thing I have to run on Sunday, and it might take a few hours, and I'm a little nervous about leaving Jack alone any more than I have to." Matt paused. He tried to judge her reaction but was uncomfortable looking her in the eyes just then. He pressed on. "And he'd like to see you again. Really. So if you don't mind, is there a chance you could maybe stop by? It wouldn't have to be for the whole two hours or anything, but—"

"I'd love to," Amanda said.

"Yeah?"

"Absolutely."

"That'd be good," Matt said. "About noon? Is that cool? I can get you some gas money or something."

"Don't worry about it. That's what friends are for. I'll see you on Sunday."

TWENTY-THREE

There were about twenty cars in front of Matt in line at the US-
Canada border checkpoint. It gave him plenty of time to think
about what he was doing.

The pickup had been no drama, no stress. Just a bored-looking
middle-aged guy, like Big Ed, at a condominium complex downtown across the street from a Tim Hortons coffee shop. He asked
Matt a few questions to verify his identity and then handed over
the box of product and directions for the stateside drop-off. Matt
stuffed the box in the trunk of the rental that Ed had set him up
with. The entire exchange had taken less than ten minutes.

That wasn't the part Matt had been worried about, anyway.
If there had been any problems on that end—sketchy guys in-
volved in the deal or whatever—and he had taken a beating, he
could have dealt with that. He'd taken a beating before.

But he couldn't deal with the fallout if the border crossing went sideways. Couldn't sit in a cage while Jack suffered alone at the trailer. He breathed deeply, trying to relax and reclaim the do-or-die clarity it had taken to make this decision. But he couldn't find it again. Right now, watching each car snake past the warning lights and stop at the booth to talk to a border patrol agent, this seemed like the stupidest thing he could possibly be doing, the worst decision he had ever made.

Matt's eyes were restless, scanning the scene in front of him. Dozens of cameras mounted on the main building and on posts along the roadway watched the cars. There were probably more cameras hidden along this route. He had heard there were all sorts of secret microphones at the border, the kinds from spy movies that could zoom in and hear conversations from long distances. He had no way of knowing whether or not that was true, but he was still grateful he was doing this job alone.

He nudged his car closer to the security booth. The line was crawling along yet moving way too fast at the same time. He was fifteen cars away. An agent in a green uniform exited the main building off to his left, leading a dog on a leash. *Shit.* How close did a drug-sniffer have to be to do its job? He watched as the guy with the dog spoke to two other agents. The dog sat at his side and stared at the line of cars.

Now he was ten cars away. Could that dog smell right through the car or did they have to open up the doors first?

Cold sweat poured from Matt's armpits and ran down his sides.

Eight cars.

The agent with the dog left the two other guys and started walking. He stopped at the security booth where Matt was in line. He and the agent there spoke briefly, then looked up and down the line of cars.

Seven.

Matt dug his fingernails into the steering wheel in a death grip. He looked in the rearview mirror, saw dozens of cars behind him. The lines of cars on either side of him stretched equally far back. There was no turning around, no backing out.

Five. Matt was close enough to see the tags on the dog's collar.

Suddenly the dog's head snapped up. *Oh no.* Was he looking at the car? *No no no no.* He was. He was looking right at Matt through the windshield. In just a minute that border agent would look around to see what the dog was staring at. And then in another thirty seconds he was going to walk right up to the car and ask Matt some questions he couldn't answer and— *Goddammit, why was that stupid dog staring at him? Why couldn't he just—*

No. A bird was flying by. The dog tracked it until it zipped out of sight, then resumed his stare into the middle distance. Matt unclenched his fists from the steering wheel.

The agent and the dog left Matt's line, walked along the row of security booths and disappeared into another building.

Matt ran over answers to the border agent's potential questions in his head. He had to make sure his voice sounded normal when he got up there. But his throat was so dry. He'd started to speak aloud, practicing, when he remembered the possibility of the hidden microphones. He shut his mouth again.

Four cars.

The SUV at the booth was taking forever. Matt had heard so many horror stories about the border, not from people in the business but from average, everyday people. The law was different here. None of that probable-cause, due-process, please-show-me-your-warrant-Mr.-Officer shit. He'd heard that they could ask you to pull over and give you absolutely no reason for it. He'd heard that they could take your car apart, literally take it apart into a million little pieces. And when they were done, even if they didn't find anything, they could just say, "Have a nice day," and you were responsible for getting your car put back together and getting out of there.

Matt tried to think about the money. If he somehow managed to get through this, he wouldn't have to worry about rent or food for a few months. And he could stock up on some meds. If only he could get past the next few minutes.

The SUV pulled away. Matt wiped his palms on his jeans.

Three cars.

He got a wild idea that the trunk had popped open all by itself, could imagine it perfectly in his mind, the trunk wide open and bouncing up and down each time he nudged the car forward. It took a great deal of willpower not to glance backward to check that it was still closed.

Two.

He was close enough to clearly see the border patrol agent, the badge he wore and the mole on his face. He waved that car through and now only one car separated Matt from the booth.

Matt forced himself to stop staring at the agent. He focused straight through the windshield and tried to control his breathing. The light turned green. Matt eased the car forward and stopped in front of the booth.

"ID."

Matt lifted his license from the front seat and handed it to the agent.

"Citizenship?"

"American."

"How long were you in Canada?"

"Couple of hours." At first Matt thought his voice was too loud, then he worried that it was too soft.

"What were you doing?"

"Just meeting a couple of friends. We saw a movie."

"Which theater?"

Matt's mind stuck in neutral for a minute. He had the name of a current movie at the ready, had the plot memorized from the trailer and knew all the actors. The agent's question was a total surprise. Seconds were ticking by. *Shit.*

"I can't remember the name. But it's the one with the rocket ship statue on top." Matt's heart raced. This was it. No way would the agent let Matt through. It was over. Would he get a phone call, at least? He realized he didn't even know where they were going to take him after they arrested him. Canada or the US? *Shit shit shit.*

"Bringing anything home with you?"

"Huh?"

The agent's eyes narrowed briefly. "Taking anything from Canada back across the border?"

"Oh. No."

The border agent handed back his license. "Drive safely."

Matt swallowed. He stared at the border agent. Thankfully his feet were quicker than his mind and he pressed on the gas pedal and eased out of the security checkpoint. One minute later he was on the freeway, driving home.

Matt counted the money in his head on the way home. He added up the time since he had left the trailer and figured out how much money he'd made by the hour. He tried not to think about how easy it would be to do it again.

TWENTY-FOUR

When Matt returned to the trailer, Amanda and Jack were sit-ting in the kitchen area, the little table covered with colored markers and Halloween cards. Jack was actually wearing a T-shirt and sweatpants instead of his bathrobe.

"Hi, Matt," Amanda said.

"You back already?" Jack said. He leaned over and stage-whispered to Amanda, "Just watch. Mr. Sunny Disposition here'll ruin all our fun now."

"Nice to see you, too, Jack." Matt took off his coat and hung it on the doorknob. He walked across the room and took a soda from the fridge. "Looks like quite the arts and crafts project you two have going there."

"We're making cards," Amanda said. "Turns out Jack has some hidden artistic talent."

But Matt noticed the bowl of food amid all the Sharpies and glue sticks. "Hey, it looks like you're branching out. Are you actually eating something besides ice cream and fish sticks?"

Jack looked down at the bowl in front of him, then winked at Amanda. "Well, sure I am. Finally got a decent cook around here."

Amanda smiled in return. "It was nothing. Just apple slices mixed with cinnamon and sugar, heated up in the microwave."

"Tasty," Jack said, waggling his eyebrows.

"And it's even good for you," Amanda said. "In the dieting world it's known as Fat Girl's Apple Pie. You should give it a try, Matt, you might like it."

The sense memory washed over Matt. His salivary glands kicked into action, filling up his mouth until he had to swallow.

"Oh, he's tried it," Jack said. "They also call it Poor Man's Apple Pie. Tell her, Matt."

Matt's face burned. "What?" He knew, of course.

"His mom," Jack said, smiling. What was up with him? He was practically bubbly. "Matt's mom used to make it all the time when he was just a little guy."

Matt hurried to change the subject. "So what're you guys doing with all these cards?"

Amanda looked sheepish but handed a Halloween card to Matt. The cartoon ghost on the cover sported a freshly drawn reddish-orange beard.

A powerful wave of nostalgia hit Matt. He remembered being a kid, when every holiday greeting card from Jack had been doctored to give the characters his signature redhead features.

Matt still had a shoe box full of those cards in the tiny bedroom closet, the only remaining mementos of his childhood; Santa Clauses with orange beards, Easter Bunnies covered in freckles, leprechauns with flaming hair spilling out from underneath their little green hats. He remembered thinking at the time that he must be the only kid in the world to get cards exactly like these.

Matt had looked forward to getting the cards so much, had read them so many times, that it still seemed weird sometimes when he saw pictures of those characters in their normal state. The traditional Santa with a white beard was not the one he had fallen in love with.

He looked at the card for a long time.

"Matt?" Amanda said. "Is everything okay? We thought that—"

"What're you just standing there for? Open it up," Jack said.

Matt blinked a few times, shaking off the memories. The caption on the front of the card read, *Happy Halloween.* Jack had added three little dots after the letters, so now it read, *Happy Halloween . . .*

Matt opened the card. A crowd of red-bearded ghosts circled the words Jack had written on the inside: *. . . from beyond the grave!* Jack had drawn a cartoon word bubble coming from one of the ghosts that said, *Boo-wahahahaha!*

Jack watched Matt's face, his eyes crinkled up in delight. When Matt closed the card Jack's slim shoulders shook with laughter. "Well?" he said between chuckles.

"I don't get it," Matt said.

"What's not to get? After I kick the bucket I'm gonna have you mail these out the last week of October. Everybody'll get a Halloween card from a real ghost!" Jack's laughter grew louder and longer until it turned into a wheezing attack. When he caught his breath he said, "Isn't that great?"

Matt tried unsuccessfully to force a smile. Thinking about a holiday without Jack was the least funny thing he could imagine. He ended up just shaking his head. "You are one morbid bastard." He didn't know whether he was kidding or not.

Jack rolled his eyes and nudged Amanda with his elbow. "I told you. His sense of humor broke when he was a kid. I ain't been able to fix it since."

Matt looked at Amanda and gestured to the marker in her hand. "And you've been encouraging him?"

"What can I say? I'm a sucker for a man who wants to color and use glitter." She and Jack shared a grin.

But her smile slipped a bit when she looked back up at Matt. "They were meant to . . . We just thought it would be funny."

Matt's whole body heated up until he felt smothered by his own clothes. "How many of these did you make, anyway?" He knew his voice was just a little too loud. He picked up a stack of the cards.

"Loads. I'm gonna have you send them to all of my friends."

"Friends?" Matt stalked to the corner and threw the half-empty soda bottle into the garbage can so hard that the can tipped over. Amanda flinched. "You've got to be fucking kidding me." His voice was much too loud for the cramped trailer now.

"What's yer problem?" Jack said.

Matt turned. "Which friends, Jack?"

Jack's smile disappeared. "I got friends."

"Really?" Matt stretched out his arms and took an exaggerated look around the little trailer. "Where are they?"

"I got friends, you little punk."

"Oh, right, it's just that they never—"

"I got lots of friends, in lots of towns." Jack was forced to stop talking by a series of harsh, dry coughs. Matt crossed his arms, fuming. He faced Amanda, eyebrows raised, and looked a question at her: *How could you be in on this?* Amanda avoided his gaze and attended to Jack, patting him during his hacking jag.

"I didn't spend my whole life in this goddamn trailer, you know," Jack said after the coughing subsided.

"Oh, I know, I know, I'm just wondering how I'm going to find all these good buddies of yours to send them your little cards." Matt hadn't realized it until this moment but his nerves were still on edge from the border crossing. "It's not like any of them ever stop by to visit, you notice that?"

"My friends don't—"

"You know what? Go on and invite some of these friends over sometime. Or—I know—maybe they could swing by around midnight and haul your ass to the bathroom and I could get some fucking sleep."

Jack growled and pushed himself out of his chair. Matt had seen that look in his eyes before. It meant someone was going to get his ass kicked.

But Jack slipped and fell back against the cheap vinyl,

coughing again. His glare intensified. He grabbed the nearest thing at hand—a glue stick—and hurled it at Matt. It bounced pitifully off his chest.

Amanda scooched her chair back. "Hey, guys. It's okay. Take it easy," she said, looking warily between the two. They ignored her.

Jack crossed his arms over his chest and glared back at Matt. "Jesus, but yer a killjoy. I'll look up the addresses myself. Shit, if you had any friends you'd understand why I was doing this in the first place."

"Oh, if I had any friends?" Matt clenched his teeth together but the words came spilling out anyway. "Yeah, it's real easy to make friends when I spend all of my time taking care of *you*."

Jack flinched as if he'd been slapped. Matt hated himself, hated that he couldn't take the words back. Hated that he didn't know if he even wanted to.

"Matt?" Amanda said. "I don't think you should—"

"Oh, so now you don't want me here, huh? That it?" Jack's throat was going dry, his voice raspy. "That's not what you were sayin' when yer mom left. You were just a scared-shitless kid."

Matt glanced at Amanda, the embarrassment making his anger more intense. "In case you haven't noticed, I'm older now, Jack. I can take care of myself."

"Well, so can I. I don't need you." Jack rose out of his chair, grunting with the effort. "I *never* needed you." He tried to storm away, but his body failed him and he ended up shambling off-kilter down the hall to the bedroom.

Matt was caught between wanting to help him down the hall and the desire to shove him the rest of the way with both hands. When the door closed, it was a pale imitation of a slam, but Matt flinched anyway.

Amanda slowly stood up. "I better get going," she said. Her voice was tight, on the verge of breaking.

"Here," Matt said. He reached into his pocket and took out a wad of cash. He peeled off three fifty-dollar bills. "This is for gas."

Amanda looked at the money. "Matt, that's way too much. I can't take that."

"It's not just for gas, then, okay? It's for babysitting. For putting up with his shit for a few hours." Matt jerked his head in the direction of Jack's bedroom. "No one should have to do that."

"I came because I wanted to."

"You *wanted* to be here?" Matt looked around at the walls of the little trailer. He knew he should stop; he wanted to stop. But he didn't know how. "Then you're as fucked up as he is."

Amanda looked at the floor instead of at Matt. But she still gathered herself and spoke. "I came here because I wanted to, Matt. I like being with Jack, and I wanted to help you." Her hands were shaking, and she clasped them together.

Matt reached into his pocket, pulled out another fifty-dollar bill and added it to the three in his hand. He threw the bills at her but they fluttered to the floor. He kicked them across the linoleum at her.

Amanda lifted her head and looked down the hall at Jack's

bedroom, and then straight into Matt's eyes. She even took a step toward him. "Why are you acting like this?" Her voice might have been a little shaky, but it was loud.

"I'm not acting like anything. I am like this." Matt retreated the few steps to the front door. "You two can make as many fucking farewell cards as you want." The whole trailer shook when he slammed the door behind him.

TWENTY-FIVE

Matt walked all the way into town through a rain that was steady but misty. He walked until it got dusky enough for the streetlights to come on, and then he walked in the dark.

The anger had left him quickly. Trying to remember why he had gotten so furious was like trying to remember the details of a dream where no one had a face.

Although the anger had totally drained away, he did not feel empty. That space was filled up now with hatred, with a dull loathing for the Matt back at the trailer. Jesus, that guy was an ass. And taking out his shit on Amanda? Who does that?

He walked underneath the awnings in the shopping district, looking through the lighted windows at people. Three kids and their parents sitting in a restaurant booth. A girl showing a pair of jeans to her boyfriend. A group of friends laughing about something. Everyone connected to everyone else.

Matt knew that after Jack died, all of those people would go on with their lives, just like nothing had happened.

When Matt got back to the trailer it was pitch-black, the rain clouds completely obscuring the moon and stars. The Buick Electra was still there, a dark lump in the gravel driveway.

He stepped through the door and stomped on the carpet, shaking the water from his hair and clothes. Amanda was sitting on the couch, reading a book under the lamp.

"He's in bed," she said, standing up. "I only stayed because I was concerned about him. Don't worry, I'm leaving now."

Matt took off his jacket and tossed it on the ground. He couldn't remember ever being this tired.

"How is he?"

"He was pretty upset, Matt. Obviously," Amanda said, not looking at him. "But we found his meds and he was eventually able to get to sleep."

Matt slumped into the recliner. Amanda walked to the kitchen table, took her jacket from one of the chairs and slipped it on. She crossed to the door, reached for the handle and paused. "He wasn't trying to be a jerk or anything, you know."

Matt nodded. The nubby weave of the carpet blurred before his eyes.

"He really thought you'd like the cards." She turned to look at him. "He was just trying . . . He said you used to like getting those cards. Back, you know, when things were better."

Matt shrugged. There were no words.

Amanda opened the door, took one step out into the rain, then turned and stepped back into the trailer.

"Matt, can I give you some advice?"

He was silent.

"The last time I talked to my dad, I was so upset because he couldn't come to my school." She wiped her eyes with the back of her sleeve. "It was just this stupid picnic at the end of the year, you know? But all the other parents were there—or at least it seemed like it—and I was so embarrassed. So I got mad at him."

Amanda took a deep breath and turned back to the door. "You never know when something you say to Jack . . . is going to be the last thing you say to him."

She pulled the jacket's hood over her head and walked out the door.

TWENTY-SIX

Matt sat in the recliner all night, slipping in and out of restless sleep. He wanted to be at least semialert in case Jack woke up and needed something. Maybe it'd be one of those nights when Jack was awake for a few hours, and then Matt would get the chance to talk to him, to try to explain somehow. But Jack slept the whole night through, the first time he had done that in a long time.

Matt wasn't able to completely wake Jack up in the morning. Just enough to get his pills into him along with a couple of sips of water. Jack didn't say anything; he barely opened his eyes.

Matt brought some cereal into Jack's bedroom and ate it dry, out of the box, sitting by Jack's bed and watching him breathe.

He stayed in the room as long as possible, hating the fact that he had to leave to get to first period.

As he approached the school, Matt tried to focus. Another high-demand time was approaching—spring break—and he had a lot of business to attend to. Every one of his in-house stash spots was full, and he had a lot of distributing to do.

Matt entered the school and walked by Officer Hershey's cubbyhole on the first floor. He figured he'd give Hershey a chance to search him right away, and then hopefully he could get down to business.

But Hershey wasn't there. Matt roamed the first floor, walking by spots where the big officer sometimes stood to greet students, but he wasn't at any of them.

Matt circled back to the cluster of administrative offices on the first floor. Mr. Marsh was standing outside his office sipping coffee. He waved Matt over.

"Hello there. I haven't seen you in a while, Matt."

"I've been pretty busy."

"I see, I see. So, have you given any thought to that application I gave you?"

"I've been pretty busy."

"We make time for things that are important to us, don't we, Matt?"

"I guess. I just don't know if that's for me, you know?"

Mr. Marsh glanced around at the office doors and leaned toward Matt. He spoke in a lower voice. "Speaking of time, be careful about how you spend yours today, okay?" A group of kids walked by, and Mr. Marsh slipped inside his office and closed the door.

Matt walked up the first set of stairs to Mr. Fitzsimmons's classroom. Fitzsimmons usually had a smoke right before the school day started, and Matt could retrieve some of his product there first.

When he was halfway up the stairs, someone called his name. He turned and two regular customers ran up the steps behind him.

"Hey, we been looking everywhere for you," the tall one said.

Matt eyed them warily. "What's up?"

A group of freshman girls walked down the steps and the boys were silent. After they passed, the tall one whispered, "You hear about what happened this weekend?"

"No, I just got here," said Matt. "What's going on?"

The tall one looked at the guy with the baseball cap. "You tell him."

"My sister was here all weekend," Baseball Cap said. "She's in the play and they have crazy rehearsal hours. So it's Sunday afternoon, and she's out in the hallway behind the stage, practicing her lines and making play posters or whatever the hell else they do. And she sees the dogs."

"What dogs?"

Baseball Cap leaned in eagerly. "Hershey and his cop buddies, they brought, like, five or six dogs in here, leading them all over the school. My sister says they were still here when she left and that was over three hours later."

Matt went cold all over.

"We think they were drug-sniffers," the tall one said.

Baseball Cap smacked him on the shoulder. "No shit, they were sniffers. What else would cops be doing with a bunch of dogs?"

"Anyway, we just wanted to tell you, bro," the tall one said. "'Cause if you get busted, there'd be a serious supply problem around here."

The warning bell rang. Students streamed up the staircase and the two regulars floated away with them.

Matt couldn't feel his feet touch the floor as he walked through the school. He didn't hear the conversations around him, either, didn't hear anything; it was like walking underwater. He ignored the bell for first period and roamed the halls alone after everyone disappeared inside their classrooms.

Matt cruised past all his stash spots. The loose paneling in the locker room had been fixed up and repainted. The oversized plastic pots with the fake plants in the student lounge had been removed. Everything was gone.

Matt did the calculations in his head. All the money he had given Big Ed for the large shipment this month was gone, no way to recover any of it. If he wanted to keep doing business he'd have to bring the stuff in every day and keep it on him at all times. Not an option. His business was crushed.

When he rounded the corner on the second floor, Mr. Gill and Officer Hershey were standing outside his first-period classroom. Hershey kept a poker face, but Gill was sporting a huge shit-eating grin.

"Good morning, Mr. Nolan," Gill said. "I hope you enjoyed your little stroll around the school grounds this morning."

Matt stopped several yards away. There was nowhere to hide, nothing to do but stand and stare at them.

Mr. Gill gestured grandly to the classroom door. "What are you waiting for? Come right in. Enjoy your public education today, Matt. I'm in such a good mood I'm not even going to give you a detention for being tardy."

Matt stood his ground. Mr. Gill looked at his watch and said, "Well, I've got a lot to do today. Better get cracking." He walked down the hall past Matt, then stopped just behind him. "You're through making me look like a jackass in my own school," he said to the back of Matt's head. "You're finished. And you know what? No one will even remember you were here at all." Then he strode down the hall and out of sight.

There was no anger in Matt. No feeling of any kind. He was totally numb.

He walked toward the classroom door on autopilot. Hershey was still there.

"You got lucky, Matt."

Matt stared through the big officer. "Right." He pushed by Hershey to open the door but the officer placed a hand on his shoulder, stopping him.

"I'm serious, Matt. There were lots of ways Gill wanted this to go down that ended with you doing time. He wanted you red-handed but couldn't get around the entrapment laws."

Matt stood there, rigid. Hershey watched him. Finally, Matt said, "Can I go now?"

Hershey sighed, lifted his palms in a what-can-you-do gesture. "Look, I shouldn't be telling you this stuff. But I want you to understand you got lucky and it won't happen again." Matt looked over Hershey's shoulder, his face blank. "This is your last chance to turn yourself around, Matt. You need to decide if you're going to be the one in control of your life, or if you're going to get nailed and let somebody else do it."

Matt waited until Hershey gave up and walked away, and then he opened the classroom door.

TWENTY-SEVEN

Matt walked home after school. He nearly got hit by passing cars several times as he zigzagged back and forth over the white line at the edge of the road. He ignored the blaring horns and the shouted insults.

Entering the trailer park, he tuned out the jokes from the picnic table regulars. When he arrived at trailer #6, he stared at the Buick Electra in the gravel driveway as he walked to the door.

Jack was curled up in a blanket on the recliner, snoring softly. Amanda sat on the couch with a book. "Hey," Matt whispered. "What're you doing here?"

"Jack asked me to come by again. Last night, while you were out." Amanda went right back to reading her book. "He asked for my help, and I'm not going to let the fact that *you* live here stop me from giving it to him."

"Oh." Matt stood in the doorway, looking around the trailer. He felt like an intruder. "How long have you been here?"

"I drove over at lunch, and then ended up staying all afternoon. Math and social studies were just having reviews for next week's quiz, so I knew I wouldn't really miss anything." Amanda plopped the book in her lap and pointed at him, her voice rising. "Besides, Jack wants me here and you don't have the right to—"

Matt held up both hands, stopping her in midsentence. "Whoa, whoa. It's okay. It's fine that you're here." He tossed his jacket on the kitchen table and slumped down into one of the chairs. He put his elbows on his knees and rested his head in his hands, rubbing his temples. Amanda resumed reading. The silence stretched between them. Matt didn't know what else to say.

He stood up and got a soda from the fridge. "I'm home for the rest of the day. I'm not chasing you out or anything, but you can leave whenever you want."

"Jack wanted me to stick around until he woke up." She didn't look up from her book this time.

Matt took a deep breath. "Look . . . I was an ass last night."

Amanda peered at him over the edge of her book. She raised her eyebrows. Matt was silent.

"Is that an apology?" Amanda said.

"I said I was an ass, okay? What more do you want?"

"Well, I guess knowing that you're an ass is a good sign.

What's that saying? 'Admitting you have a problem is the first step on the road to recovery'? This could be your chance to recover."

"They have a twelve-step program for assholes?"

"Yeah. I think Mr. Gill teaches it."

Matt might have smiled at that had it been a different day. "I never said thanks. You know, for being here yesterday."

Amanda waited a moment. "Are you saying thanks now?"

"Jesus." Matt rolled his eyes. "Yes, okay? I am officially apologizing *and* saying thank you."

"Then you are officially forgiven—provided you don't do it again—and you're welcome."

"I'm glad you were here. It made what I had to do a little easier."

"You want to talk about that?"

"No."

"Big surprise."

Matt looked over at Jack. "How long's he been asleep?"

Amanda looked at the time. "A couple of hours. He was out when I got here, then he woke up for a little while. We had time to play half a game of cribbage before he drifted off again."

"He have anything to eat?"

Amanda shook her head. "He wouldn't touch anything. He . . . uh . . . had a little accident. You know, in his bed. He was super embarrassed, poor thing, but I helped him get cleaned up."

"Oh, Jesus." Matt covered his eyes with one hand. For some reason he was feeling embarrassed, too. "I'm so sorry about that.

Really. I can hardly ever get him to use that stupid port-a-potty. I wish you didn't—"

"It's okay, Matt. He's sick. It happens."

Matt dropped his hand and looked at Amanda. Really looked at her. "Thank you."

"Careful, Matt. That's twice in one day."

"Shut up."

Amanda smiled. "Besides, I figure now I have something to say during my next nursing interview. That was some real-world experience right there."

"I bet." Matt sighed. "Anything else I should know?"

"Let's see . . . oh, he was having trouble swallowing his pills, so I ground them up into powder and dissolved them in a little bit of water. It was all he could do to get that down."

"That's a good idea. I'll have to try that."

They were quiet together after that. More reading and some homework for Amanda. Lots of staring at the walls for Matt. When the sun went down they silently put together a simple dinner. They ate on the couch, near Jack, hoping he would wake up and be able to eat a few bites. But he snored the entire time.

Amanda left around 9 p.m. on the condition that Matt would give her an update on Jack the next day. Matt let her go without telling her that there was no point in his being at school anymore.

Matt sat on the coffee table in front of Jack and watched him sleep. Jack's cheeks were sunken, there was no denying that. And his skin looked bad; his beard was getting patchy and there was a splotchy red rash growing underneath it, as if the whiskers were finally irritating his face after so many years there.

Matt desperately wanted Jack to wake up. He wanted to apologize. He wanted to talk, or maybe just sit there with Jack and watch something on TV. He glanced at the clock and calculated that Jack had been awake for less than an hour, total, in the last twenty-four hours.

It struck him suddenly that this could be it. At some point, Jack was going to close his eyes and not open them again. It could be today. He knew it was possible, but it didn't seem fair. What about a real goodbye? What about the shit people said on their deathbed that their family and friends never forgot, that changed their lives somehow?

Matt realized he wasn't going to get any warning. It was just going to happen when it happened.

Restless, he roamed around the trailer with a trash bag, dumping out ashtrays and picking up pizza boxes and the used tissues Jack dropped all over the place. He tidied up the kitchen and got the medicine cabinet in order. Maybe the place didn't have to be such a pit when Jack woke up.

If Jack woke up.

TWENTY-EIGHT

When Jack started calling out for Cassie, Matt was sitting on the floor, resting against the couch. It was still dark outside and Matt jerked awake at the sound of Jack's voice, disoriented. Hearing his mom's name like that made it even more difficult to tell where he was, what was going on.

"Cassie? Where are you, Cassie?"

Matt wiped his mouth on his sleeve and got his bearings. The recliner was empty, Jack's blanket strewn across the floor. Matt stood up on tired legs and looked around. The trailer was dimly lit by the light in the hallway.

"Cassie? We got to leave in the morning, girl. Got to leave real early. Come on, now."

Jack was in the corner of the dark kitchen area fumbling at the wall like he was trying to open a door that wasn't there. He turned, bumped into a chair, then groped his way back to his spot in the corner.

Matt approached Jack slowly. He put his hand on Jack's shoulder and gently turned him around.

"Cassie? That you?"

"No, Jack, it's me. I'm right here."

Jack squinted at Matt, studying him. Matt saw no recognition in his eyes.

The ache in Matt's chest surprised him; how overwhelming it was and especially how quickly it hit him. Not having Jack know who he was *hurt*. It hurt worse than the way Matt had imagined it would feel when Jack died.

"Where is she? You know Cassie?"

Matt placed one hand on his uncle's back and took him by the elbow to lead him away from the kitchen area. "I know Cassie," Matt said. He wanted his voice to be soothing but knew it sounded forced, raw. "But she's not here right now. Let's get you to bed." Matt led Jack around the kitchen table, then slowly walked him through the living room.

"Tell her we're leavin' in the morning, leavin' early," Jack said. He shuffled along beside Matt, his hands up to protect himself, like a blind man. "You tell her I'll take care of it. Take care of all of it."

"I will," Matt whispered. "I'll tell her that." He walked Jack down the hallway toward the bedroom.

"I'll take care of everything," Jack said.

Matt guided Jack into the bedroom and helped him sit down on the edge of the bed. He clicked on the bedside lamp and pushed some magazines off the bed so Jack would have room to lie down. Matt knelt in front of Jack to take off his slippers.

"Big Matty?"

Matt's breath caught in his throat when he heard the name Jack used to call him when he was a little kid. "Is that you, Big Matty?"

Matt looked up to see Jack squinting down at him. He swallowed heavily and nodded. "Yeah. It's me, Uncle Jack."

"Look at you, Big Matty. Yer sure growin' up." Jack reached out and let his hand fall on top of Matt's head. He rubbed his hand around, messing up Matt's hair, just like he did when Matt was a little kid. Matt took off Jack's slippers and slipped them under the bed while Jack patted him.

Jack let his hand fall away. "You seen yer mother anywhere? I'm lookin' for her."

"She's not here right now, Uncle Jack."

"Okay."

Jack sat there for a minute, gazing at the wall. A smile played across his lips for a moment, and Matt wished he knew what Jack was seeing.

Even though Jack was in his own world, his own time, Matt forged ahead with what he had been waiting to tell him. He knew it was probably useless, but he figured it might help on some level. And although he didn't exactly admit it to himself just then, he wanted to make sure he didn't miss his last chance.

"Jack?"

"Mmmm-hmmm?"

"I just wanted to say I'm sorry."

"Huh?"

"I'm really sorry. For what I said. You know I want you here. I've always wanted you here."

Jack shook his head. "You don't never have to say sorry to your uncle, Big Matty, you know that."

Matt nodded. The needles burned at the back of his eyes again but this time he didn't fight it.

"Thanks, Uncle Jack."

"You bet. Now, yer not so big you can't give old Uncle Jack a hug, are you?"

Matt swallowed. He hadn't hugged Jack since he was five or six years old.

Jack spread his arms wide. Matt hesitated, then moved close.

Jack let his arms, so light, fall over Matt's shoulders. Matt wrapped his arms around Jack, his cheek resting on Jack's shoulder. Underneath the smell of mentholated rub and old bathrobe and unwashed hair was the smell of Uncle Jack, unchanged over all the years. Jack patted him on the back, whispering, "Yer a good little guy, Big Matty."

"You too, Uncle Jack."

"You always been my favorite, you know. My favorite little guy in the world."

Matt didn't know how long it took before Jack's breathing got heavier, more rhythmic, finally turning to light snores. He only knew that he held on to his uncle for a long time after that.

TWENTY-NINE

Matt slept in until ten the next morning. Jack woke him up when he tried to get out of bed and knocked the bedside lamp onto the floor. Matt pulled himself off the couch, stumbled down the hallway to fetch Jack and get him into the bathroom and then got a warm bath ready for him.

Jack's mind was more alert this morning—he was back in the present day, at least—but his body was slower, more unsteady. After Jack's bath the two of them sat in the living room and watched part of an old movie on TV. Matt made fish sticks, but Jack only had two or three bites before making a face and pushing the plate away. Nothing else Matt suggested sounded good to him. By eleven o'clock Jack asked to go back to bed.

...

Matt was lying on the couch, staring blankly at the TV, when he heard the crunch of tires on the driveway gravel. He sighed, pushed himself off the couch and opened the front door.

"How's Jack?" Amanda said.

"Good morning to you, too."

"It's noon, Matt. Is Jack okay?"

Matt shrugged. "He was up for a little while, earlier. He's back in bed now. But he's as okay as he can be, I guess."

"Then what are you doing here? Why aren't you at school?"

Matt stepped back, pushing the door wide open. "I suppose you're going to want to come in."

Amanda pushed past him, stood in the living room and crossed her arms. "Why aren't you at school?"

Matt took a deep breath. "Amanda . . . I think I'm pretty much done with school."

"Does this have to do with those police dogs messing with your little business operation?"

Matt raised his eyebrows. "You heard about that?"

"I might be a social outcast, Matt, but I'm not deaf. Everybody heard about that."

Matt raised both palms for a moment. "Then, yeah. That's the reason."

"Well, Matt, that's about the stupidest thing I've ever heard." Amanda kept her eyes steadily on Matt's.

"People don't talk to me like that."

"I'm not one of your customers."

"Ex-customers. Besides, I can't go. He needs me here."

"What he needs is to know that you're going to be okay after he's gone. That you're not going to be some degenerate high school dropout."

"You have no fucking idea what he needs. Just leave us alone." Matt marched to the door and pushed it open.

Amanda took off her coat, slowly, deliberately, and laid it over the back of a kitchen chair. Then she sat down, took her math book out of her backpack and started doing homework.

She'd worked for a few moments when she said, without looking up, "Lunch period will be over in fifteen minutes. You can still make it to school in time for afternoon classes. I can afford to skip a few times, but I'm guessing you can't."

Matt stood by the open door, continuing to watch her. A minute or so later she looked up and said, "You're not going to do this alone, Matt. Get used to it. I'm going to watch out for Jack today." She bent her head back to her work and added, "You can either go back to school or stand there and stare at the wall, but either way, please close the door. It's getting drafty in here."

Matt sighed, shook his head and walked out the door of the trailer.

After that day, Matt and Amanda fell into a caretaking routine. Amanda switched a couple of her classes over to Independent Study so she could spend more time at the trailer during the day. Matt feigned illness during the classes where he could recoup lost points by making up tests and projects at home, and tried as much as he could to attend the classes that counted daily participation points. It was easier than arguing with Amanda. He also attended the Helping Hands meetings, doing work for Ms. Edwards, while Amanda finished up the book drive on Saturday afternoons. Between the two of them, they managed to have someone with Jack at the trailer almost all the time.

Matt thought he'd kept a low profile at school before, dodging security cameras, flying under the radar of busy teachers. But now he knew what it felt like to be truly invisible. No one spoke to him. Sure, someone might say hello when passing on a staircase or give him a nod of recognition in the halls, but not one of the people he used to talk to sought him out for any reason. Rumor had it that one of the juniors, a recent transfer from a bigger school down south, had stepped in to fill the void in the black market left by Matt's forced retirement.

Matt made a couple more trips across the border for Big Ed. His nerves at the border crossing got worse, but Matt knew he had to deal with it, just part of the job. Money was no longer a problem.

Jack deteriorated. The times he spent awake got further and further apart and lost all semblance of a regular schedule. The times when he was both awake and lucid were even rarer. He often spoke of people and places from his past. Many times, Matt could not understand the words at all.

Jack ate less each day. Even though Matt wouldn't have believed it possible, Jack somehow lost even more weight. He stopped going into the living room and spent his days and nights in the bedroom. Matt bought a foam pad and spread it out next to the bed and slept there each night.

Jack hardly ever needed to go to the bathroom anymore, but whenever he did he used the portable toilet. Matt had to lift him out of bed, Jack clutching feebly at his shoulders, and set him on the potty. Often Jack would fall asleep sitting there, without having done anything. Matt learned the hard way to leave him there until he woke up again and did his business; otherwise he just went in his bed. Matt left a magazine or some handouts from his classes and a flashlight in the bedroom. He frequently sat and read, sometimes for an hour or two in the middle of the night, while Jack dozed on the portable toilet or stared slack-jawed at the wall.

One night Matt was sitting on the bed, reading an old copy of *Sports Illustrated*. Jack had been dozing on the potty for over an hour. Matt read the same paragraph over and over, trying to stay awake. He sat very close, didn't want Jack to roll off and hurt himself. It had been over two days since Jack had said a word that Matt could understand.

"Matt," Jack said, clear as anything.

Matt dropped the magazine and looked at his uncle. Jack's eyes were fixed on Matt, totally alert, searching his face. Matt couldn't hold back an irrational surge of hope that Jack was getting better. It only lasted a moment. "Yeah, Jack?"

Jack sighed heavily. He fixed Matt with his stare. "You never told me it was going to be like this."

Matt's eyes burned. His breath caught in his throat before he was able to force the words out in a whisper. "I'm sorry, Jack. I didn't know. I'm so sorry."

But Jack's face had gone slack again, and the light faded from his eyes. He dozed on the potty for another half hour before nature took over. Matt cleaned him up and eased him back into bed.

THIRTY

Matt and Amanda were playing cards in the living room on a Saturday morning when they heard Jack tapping his spoon against the lamp in the bedroom. They walked down the hall together.

Jack tried to speak but all that came out was a raspy wheeze. Matt and Amanda had both found that the best way to deal with this was to sit beside him on the bed and speak soothingly to him until he gave up the effort and fell back asleep. It usually didn't take long.

But his wheezing went on and on this time. He became agitated.

"I think he's really trying to tell us something," Amanda said. "Prop him up. I'll get some water."

Matt lifted Jack up and wedged some pillows behind his shoulders. Amanda helped him sip at a glass of water.

"Thanks," Jack whispered. He sipped a little more. "I need something."

"What, Jack?"

"Pencil . . . pad a paper." Jack rested, collected himself. "Need to write."

Matt rummaged through the drawers in the kitchen and brought Jack what he needed. Matt sat on the bed, Amanda in a chair, while Jack pressed the pencil to the paper. Jack paused and looked up at them. "Guy needs . . . little privacy."

"No problem," Matt said. He and Amanda went back into the living room.

Matt assumed that Jack would fall asleep, but half an hour later Jack tapped his spoon again and they returned to the bedroom. Jack was clutching a piece of yellow legal-sized paper in one hand. "Envelope," he whispered. When Matt complied, Jack folded up the paper as best he could, his hands trembling, and with a concentrated effort managed to shove the paper into the envelope. His tongue was too dry to moisten the sticky flap enough to keep it closed. Amanda stepped in and did it for him, neatly sealing the envelope.

"Thanks, dear," Jack said. He motioned for Matt to come closer. Matt knelt on the edge of the bed. "Need a favor," Jack said.

"Anything."

"Need you . . . take this . . . to your mother."

Matt pressed his mouth into a line. He instinctively glanced over at Amanda for a second, then leaned into Jack and lowered his voice. "Jack, we've talked about this before. You know I don't want—"

Jack lifted one hand from the bed, cutting Matt off. "Sorry, kid . . . guy in the deathbed . . . makes the rules." He smiled at that and for an instant looked like the Jack that Matt remembered.

Matt stared at the envelope in his hands. He didn't look up when he mumbled, "I'll do it. I'll do it for you."

Jack shook his head. He reached out and touched Matt's hand until Matt looked him in the eye again. "No. Do it . . . for you."

Matt drove the Buick Electra for over an hour on the freeway until he spotted the green sign with white letters. STATE CORRECTIONAL FACILITY.

The squat gray building sat all by itself, surrounded by miles of fields and farmland. Matt eased the car through the gate in the twenty-foot security fence. He pulled up to the guards' station.

Matt answered a series of questions, and Amanda's car was briefly searched. He parked in the visitors' lot, then walked through another security fence to the main building.

The faded checkerboard floor tile, drab white walls and strips of fluorescent lighting all reminded him of high school. He filled out a form at reception, showed his driver's license, then underwent a brief frisking. It didn't take long; all he had was the clothes he was wearing and Jack's letter.

Matt was led to the visitors' room, a square, featureless area with small tables and chairs spaced evenly throughout. He was half an hour early for visiting hours and the room was empty. He sat at one of the tables and waited.

He folded his hands on the table and kept his eyes focused there, but it was impossible to block out the memories of this room; the first time he had visited, so angry at his mom that he had hardly been able to look at her. The lame explanations and excuses for the shit she did were so much less convincing here than they had been at home.

For the first couple of years that Matt had lived with Jack, his uncle had insisted that he visit at least once every three months. Maybe if he had been a little kid at the time, it might have worked. He might have been happy for the chance to at least see his mom. But he was thirteen then, too angry to even try to enjoy the visits. When he turned sixteen, Jack said he could make up his own mind. Matt hadn't been back since.

Eventually the room started filling up. Three women who looked to be in their twenties gathered at one table. An elderly woman with three small children, the kids arguing noisily in Spanish. A middle-aged man, alone. Matt glanced at the clock. With two minutes to go until visiting hours, nearly all the tables were filled up.

Matt knew the drill. The thick security door buzzed and a guard in a green uniform stepped through. Behind him, standing single file in the hallway beyond, were the female prisoners. Only the first one in line was visible, though, a slim Latina woman in dull blue prison garb. The guard stood at the door and waved her through, and she walked to the elderly woman and the three children, who mobbed her. The elderly woman stood up on her toes to kiss the woman's cheek while the kids clutched fiercely at her legs, the tallest one reaching up to hug her around the waist. The prisoner smiled and managed to wade through everyone and sit down, the kids immediately piling onto her lap.

The next woman in line stepped forward. She had frizzy hair and dark circles under her eyes, and even though she looked like she was in her forties, there were way too many lines on her face. The guard nodded and she drifted off to one of the tables in the back of the room.

Matt watched as each woman entered the room to find her family or friends. Totally against his will, a surge of hope rushed through him. But hope for what? That she would have figured anything out? That she actually had some sort of a plan for after she got released? That she'd be so glad to see him that maybe they could have a real conversation? He wasn't sure. He tried to hold on to the anger, to keep it in the front of his mind. It should have been easier to do.

One by one, the women kept entering and sitting at the tables. Soon the entire room was filled with a soft roar of conversation. Matt watched as a heavyset woman entered and sat down with the middle-aged man. Then the guard pushed the door until it clanged shut.

Matt looked around, confused. Had he missed her?

He stood and walked to the guard. "Hey, I was waiting for someone. Has there been, I don't know, some kind of mistake?"

"Name?"

"Matt Nolan."

"No, the name of the inmate."

"Cassie—Cassandra Nolan."

The guard looked at the clipboard he was holding. "Nolan . . . Nolan . . . let me see." He flipped through several pages. "I don't see . . . oh, wait, here it is." The guard frowned, then looked up at Matt. "Cassandra Nolan lost her visiting day privileges this month. Disciplinary action." He looked at his clipboard again. "She'll be eligible to receive visitors again three weeks from today." All the air left Matt. He couldn't speak, just looked at the guard. "Sorry, guy. Do you have anything you'd like to leave for her? I can make sure she gets it."

Matt looked at the envelope in his hand. He shook his head, stuffed the letter in his pocket, then turned and walked through the door for civilians.

Matt stalked back to the car, his vision narrowed down to one little pinprick of light just ahead of him.

The anger burned through his body, but not for his mother. The anger was for himself, for being stupid enough to believe, for even a second, in a glimmer of hope. To wish for even a second that things might be different. He should have known that Cassie Nolan could figure out how to be absent even when she was a captive audience, that she could manage to be a shitty mother, even on visiting day.

Matt sat behind the wheel of the Buick for several minutes, not quite trusting himself to drive yet.

He pulled the bent envelope from his pocket. He felt a twinge of guilt for ripping the flap open, but it quickly passed. Maybe something in there could help him give Jack what he needed as he neared the end. Or maybe there was something that could help Matt understand, even a tiny bit, how his mother could have ended up like this.

He removed the yellow paper, his heart racing for some reason. He unfolded the letter and . . . nothing. Just a mishmash of meaningless scribbles, like when toddlers first pretend to write.

Matt crumpled up the paper and tossed it out the window before driving away.

THIRTY-ONE

Another week passed. During the rare times when Jack was co-herent for a few moments, he didn't ask about the trip to the prison. Matt didn't remind him.

Matt had trouble sleeping. He usually stayed up all night watching Jack and then dozed for a couple of hours at a time in the afternoons when Amanda was there.

Neither Matt nor Amanda could get Jack to swallow his medicine, but there was no noticeable effect, no more screaming pain fits. He was in a place beyond pain.

One night, a couple of hours after Amanda had left, Matt was reading a magazine on the floor beside Jack's bed. Jack drew in a long, shaky breath. And then there was silence.

Matt lay on the floor, waiting for the next breath. When it

didn't come he got up on his knees and looked at Jack. He lay there, his face completely slack, totally silent.

So this is what it looks like. Death. Matt was dazed. There was no sadness, no relief. Just watching Jack lie there. He did not think of it yet as Jack's body.

And then Jack shattered the silence, sucking in a loud, raspy breath. Matt flinched, and the sadness was there, overwhelming him. And finally, the tears.

Jack was quiet again, not breathing, for five seconds. Ten. Fifteen. Matt didn't breathe, either, waiting. He thought this must be it when Jack pulled in another ragged, horrible breath.

It continued all night, the impossibly long pauses interrupted by short bursts of tortured wheezing. Matt watched Jack die a thousand times that night.

The light that filtered in through the blinds was gray when Jack stopped breathing for the final time. During the pause afterward, Matt waited for the next wheeze to rip up his heart some more. The silence stretched for several minutes before Matt admitted to himself that it really was over this time.

He was going to reach out and touch Jack, but when he looked down he realized that he was holding Jack's hand, had been holding it all night.

THIRTY-TWO

Matt sat on the edge of the bed for a long time. He didn't know yet how he was supposed to feel. He wasn't any sadder than he had been yesterday, or last week. He just felt dazed.

When he finally got up, he pulled the quilt over Jack's face. He plodded down the hall into the kitchen area. He stared at the fridge and the cupboards, uncomprehending. He couldn't remember the last time he had eaten anything, or even what the desire to eat felt like.

He lowered himself onto a kitchen chair and stared at the trailer. It seemed different this morning. Before, it had been so tiny, so cramped. He and Jack had always been bumping into each other, competing for storage space and breathing room, before Jack had gotten sick. As Matt grew bigger throughout his teenage years, the trailer had seemed to be shrinking around him, suffocating him.

Now it was cavernous.

Matt thought about getting up, moving to the couch, but that seemed like it would require too much effort. Grief had not taken over his mind yet—maybe it was too soon—but it had definitely settled into his body. He felt sluggish to the point of paralysis.

He slowly lifted his head and looked at the clock. Again. It was only two minutes later than the last time he had checked.

He went over the numbers in his head. Amanda's last morning class would be over in nine minutes. It would take at least five minutes to get the Buick out of the student parking lot, given the lunchtime rush. Then five more to drive to the trailer park. Throw in a few more minutes because she wasn't the fastest walker in the world. But half an hour should be a safe guess. Another half hour and he wouldn't have to be alone anymore.

Part of Matt's mind was disgusted for this weakness. For thinking that being around another person would help, for allowing himself to form a bond with someone when those bonds always fell apart, one way or another.

He told that part of his mind to shut the fuck up. Amanda had earned the right to be here today.

■ ■ ■

When Matt heard tires crunching through the gravel of the trailer park road he pushed himself out of his seat and looked out the kitchen window, even though only a couple of minutes had passed and it was way too early for her to show up. But it was just the old pickup truck from three trailers down. Matt shook his head, couldn't believe he was acting like some kind of damn puppy.

When the next two cars drove through the park Matt stayed at the kitchen table, waiting to hear if one of them would stop at the trailer. He told himself to play it cool but he couldn't control his heart, which sped up when the cars got near. But both of them just drove on past.

Matt moved to the couch. He lay down, and even though he didn't feel tired, the sheer exhaustion from having stayed up each night to watch Jack took over and he fell asleep.

A knock on the door jerked him instantly awake from a deep sleep. Two thoughts hit him simultaneously. The first was *Jack is dead,* and the realization was a hard, cold lump in the middle of his belly. The second was *She's finally here.* This thought surprised and frightened him. He'd thought he was used to being alone, that he could handle it. But this was different. This wasn't the alone that he felt at school, surrounded by people who didn't matter. He always had Jack back at the trailer, so being alone at school was a choice, part of the necessary barrier between him and the idiots he had to deal with there.

Now that Jack was gone, the aloneness had changed. It was inside him now. It was feeding on whatever it could find in there, until Matt felt emptier and emptier. Even though he knew it was ridiculous to feel this way, he wanted to see Amanda to make sure he didn't disappear.

Matt rolled off the couch and opened the front door. Standing outside was Janice, smacking her gum and holding her cigarette.

"Hey, kid," she said.

Matt just stared at her.

Janice tilted her head and raised her eyebrows. She gestured with the cigarette hand, palm up, and waited for Matt to say something. Eventually, she said, "First of the month. Ringin' any bells?"

Matt turned, leaving Janice standing outside, and walked mechanically to the closet. He found his jar, stuffed full of cash, and pulled out the necessary bills. He returned to the doorway and held them out to Janice.

"I didn't used to have to remind you so much, ya know," Janice said, pocketing the bills. She looked back up at him and her eyes softened around the edges, then crinkled up in concern. "You doin' okay, kid?"

Matt nodded.

"You sure?" Janice tilted her head again. "You, uh, you need anything?"

"No."

Matt shut the door. He returned to the couch to lie down, but sleep did not come to him again.

THIRTY-THREE

Matt checked the clock less and less frequently. When nearly two hours had passed since the final bell of the school day, he admitted to himself that Amanda wasn't going to show up.

The anger helped. It rushed in like a wave and washed away all the useless emotions. Sadness and self-pity and fear. What good was it to ever feel shit like that?

The anger helped sharpen his thinking. You can only count on yourself. If you expect someone else to help you through the shit, it's only going to get worse.

The anger helped him focus. There was stuff he had to do, and it wasn't going to get done if he sat around here feeling sorry for himself. The anger helped him shake off the sluggishness and stand up, then rummage around in the kitchen drawers until he found the phone book.

He sat back at the kitchen table and pawed through the yellow pages. *Food Banks . . . Foster Care . . . Freezers . . . Fumigating . . . Funeral Services.*

Matt was disgusted by the cheesy pictures on the advertisements. A soft golden sunset over a cluster of islands in the bay. A wreath of flowers surrounded by candles. Three generations of a family-owned business, standing around in suits with camera smiles frozen on their faces. Why did everything have to be so fucking fake?

Matt skipped all those, found a place with a simple ad, no pictures and no bullshit. Just the name, After Care Funeral Home and Cremation Services, an address and a phone number.

Matt picked up the phone, started to push the numbers, put the phone down again.

He walked slowly down the hall. He had closed the door to the bedroom and he stood in front of it now. He thought he was going to open it up, but he just placed his palm on the door. He slowly leaned forward until his forehead was resting on the wood.

He stood that way for a long time, trying to gather up his will to make the phone call. Saying goodbye.

Eventually, he walked back to the kitchen, pulled out his phone and dialed the number.

Matt was sitting by the window when the van drove up. He opened the door to the funeral workers.

"Hello, I'm Greg from After Care," the one with dark hair

said, his features appropriately composed. "Are you Matt No-lan?" Matt nodded. "I'm so sorry for your loss, Matt." Matt just stood there. Greg spoke in a lower voice. "We're here to pick up Jack."

Matt pushed the door open for them and stepped back into the trailer.

Greg paused. "Maybe you'd like to get a little air, Matt. Maybe take a short walk around outside?"

"He's down the hall, in the bedroom." Matt didn't move.

Greg from After Care cleared his throat. "It's really for the best, Matt, I can assure you. If you'd leave the premises, just for a short while. This part can be upsetting. Maybe you could—"

"Just do what you have to fucking do."

Greg glanced at his partner, who nodded once. Matt sat on the couch, his arms crossed over his chest.

The two men walked down the hall. They didn't speak while they worked, but Matt could hear them fumbling around in the bedroom.

When they walked back through the living room, each man was carrying one end of a black body bag. Matt stared at it. There was no way the tiny bulge was big enough to be Jack, no way that bag could ever contain him.

Matt wished he had listened to them and left the trailer.

A few hours later, Matt walked back down the hall. The bedroom door had been left open.

The funeral home guys had made the bed, every corner

tucked in, every pillow in place. The bed had never been this neat, not ever, and there was no sign left that Jack had spent so many nights there. Matt was so furious that he slammed his fist into the door. The thin wood crumpled and splintered under his fist, but he didn't punch all the way through. There was just a big, jagged dent in the middle of the door.

Matt closed the door and walked back to the living room and sat on the couch. The trailer grew dark around him.

He was still there when the trailer park regulars stopped their hooting and hollering and drifted one by one back to their trailers. He was still there when the gray light of a new day filtered in through the windows.

THIRTY-FOUR

When the trailer park started stirring again, front doors slam- ming and cars driving across the gravel, headed for town, Matt made coffee and poured a bowl of cereal. Not because he was hungry, but because that was what people did in the morning.

He sat at the kitchen table for a long time. There was no reason to get up. No medicines to fetch, no schedule to keep. Nothing.

A few minutes after breakfast, or maybe four or five hours, there was a knock on the door. Amanda stood on the gravel outside. When Matt opened the door she was rummaging around in a grocery bag. "I brought something for you," she said. She found something at the bottom of the bag and pulled it out. It was a box of adult diapers. "Before you say no, just give these a chance. It'll be better than cleaning up the bed, plus we can always—" Amanda looked up at Matt's face then, and instantly her expression changed. Her eyes grew round and her mouth opened, and then her whole face contracted in concern. "Oh, Matt, I'm so sorry." Tears welled up in her eyes.

Amanda dropped the box and the grocery bag and moved toward Matt with her arms open. He held one hand up and stopped her.

She pulled back immediately, then wiped at her eyes with her sleeve. "I'll give the funeral people a call, okay? We can take a walk or something while they come over. Maybe down to the riverside or the park or somewhere." She searched his face. "Okay?"

"They already came by. Yesterday."

Amanda's face crumpled. "I didn't get a chance to say goodbye." She buried her face in her hands, sobbing.

They stood that way for a long time, Amanda crying, Matt standing there and looking out over the trailer park.

When Amanda's sobs leveled off, she took some tissue out of her purse and cleaned up her face.

"Do you want to take a drive? Go to a restaurant or something? We don't have to eat or anything, we could just sit there and talk. Or not talk, and drink coffee. It would just be, you know, somewhere to be. Somewhere else."

Matt shook his head. He still didn't look at her.

Amanda studied his face. "Matt, is there . . . I almost said 'Is there anything wrong?' but that's a stupid thing to say right now." She paused for a few moments, clearly to let Matt speak if he was going to. "But is there . . . is there anything else?"

Matt avoided eye contact and shook his head.

"Matt, don't do this," Amanda whispered. "Don't go back to the way it was before. Don't go back to the way you were."

"Not going back. Always been like this."

Amanda shook her head. "That's not true, Matt. You know you—"

"You weren't here!" Matt blurted out. Amanda took a step backward, as if she'd been slapped. "You weren't here when I needed you. You're just like everyone else."

Amanda opened her mouth to speak, but no words came out. Matt glared at her for a few moments, then turned and walked back into the trailer. He had moved to shut the door when Amanda put her palm against it, holding it open.

"Matt, I had to go to my afternoon classes and then meet with my Independent Study advisors after school. They had to check my work and sign a bunch of forms. Then I had to help my mom go shopping in the evening. I told you all that!"

"No, you didn't."

Amanda's hand fell from the door. She stared at Matt as he took another step backward. "Then maybe I forgot. Or maybe you forgot I told you. It's been so crazy lately. But none of that matters. I'm here *now*, Matt. I'll stay as long as you need me to. And then I'll come back tomorrow. And the day after that."

Matt retreated farther into the dim interior of the trailer. "Don't worry about it. He's dead, you know? I don't need help anymore."

"Matt . . . I don't think that's true."

"I don't need anything." Matt stepped forward and closed the door.

He stood there for a long time, staring at the door. The Buick hadn't driven away yet, so he knew she was still out there. After a long time he heard her call to him, "You don't have to be alone."

She didn't know that it wasn't a choice. He was alone.

THIRTY-FIVE

Matt started to take long walks. No direction, no destination, just one foot in front of the other.

He set out at the time when he normally would have gone to school. By lunchtime he would reach one of the neighboring small towns, where he would stop and chew on a tasteless burger at a fast-food place, head bent over his food at a booth in the corner. Afterward he would walk around town and then back home, sometimes getting there before dark, sometimes not. When he finally crashed on the couch in the evenings—he never used the bed in the bedroom—the physical exhaustion would pull him under and he'd be able to get some kind of sleep. He had learned that if he made himself tired enough, he wouldn't have to think about anything.

THIRTY-SIX

Amanda came by every evening. At first she knocked on the door, quietly but insistently, for a long time. When she got tired of knocking, she would say, "You don't have to go through this by yourself." It was easy to hear her through the thin walls of the trailer.

After the first week of Matt not opening the door, she gave up on the knocking altogether. Instead she parked her car in the driveway and read a book by flashlight. She stayed there for two or three hours at a time, sometimes even longer. Matt could see her, framed by the kitchen window, when he got a glass of water, or through the tiny bathroom window when he stood at the toilet. Sometimes he peeked around the curtain in the living room before hitting the couch for the night. It was easier to get to sleep on the nights when she was still out there.

THIRTY-SEVEN

A few weeks after Jack's death, Matt opened the door to the bedroom for the first time. It looked very small.

He brought a trash bag and a cardboard box. He tossed all the medicines and tissues and other reminders of Jack's illness in the trash bag. In the box, he carefully placed the rest of Jack's things, the clothes from the drawers, his watch and wallet and some jewelry and other things. He found a piece of scratch paper where Amanda and Jack had recorded the winnings from their cribbage games, Amanda way out in front. Matt put this into the box.

Without quite knowing what he was doing at first, Matt started to search the room, looking in the very back of the drawers of the bedside table, behind the headboard, potential little hiding places. He was looking for something that Jack might have left him, a note or a picture or something. It was exactly the kind of thing Jack would do. Matt could just see him, sitting in bed alone, thinking about Matt finding a little posthumous surprise and grinning his ass off. Matt could picture it perfectly, and it made the hollow place in his heart ache.

But Matt couldn't find anything like that. Jack was gone.

THIRTY-EIGHT

Big Ed called about more border crossings, and Matt went just to have something to do. He did not need the money.

He felt nothing the entire time, just a dull calmness as he waited in line at the border and spoke to the agent at the booth. He didn't think this would change even if they asked him to pull over and found the box of product in the trunk. He would just go where they told him to go, do what they told him to do. The idea of prison stopped being scary. Became almost comforting. Inmates didn't have to think about the future.

The border agents never asked him more than a question or two before waving him through. Matt couldn't help feeling a little disappointed as he drove back to the trailer.

THIRTY-NINE

One night Matt had the dream. Jack's car dream. The one where Jack was stuck on a long, dark road. But he didn't think about Jack; the dream wasn't about Jack. It was Matt in the car.

The only difference was how fast he was going. There was the same feeling of being trapped, the same total lack of control, the same stark fear of where he was headed. But he was flying on the way there, road signs whipping by in a blur as he rushed toward the blackness.

Matt was usually able to empty his mind on his long walks, take some comfort in the mindless repetition of one foot in front of the other. But after the dream he had to give them up. Didn't want to spend all that time on a road again. Couldn't risk facing that feeling when he was awake.

FORTY

That evening, or maybe an evening some weeks later, someone knocked on the door. Loudly.

Matt nudged the curtain aside and saw Amanda's Buick in the driveway. He stayed on the couch.

"Matt, please open the door." More knocking. "Please."

Matt almost said "Go away," but his throat felt rusty with disuse. He didn't know if it would work.

Eventually, the knocking stopped. But when she spoke again, her voice was louder. Stronger. "He made me promise to wait until Halloween. That was going to be his big joke. But I think you should have this now."

Matt looked at the door. An envelope slipped underneath and lay on the faded carpet.

A few minutes later the gravel crunched under the tires as the Buick left.

Matt stared at the envelope for a long time. When he finally got up to take it, his head was very light. He felt like he was floating across the small living room.

He didn't open the envelope and remove the card until he'd walked over to the kitchen table. When he saw the doctored illustration on the front—a group of ghosts sporting orange beards, flaming hair and red-Sharpie freckles all over their arms—his legs collapsed, and he slumped down into one of the chairs.

His hands trembling, he opened the card. It was filled with Jack's unmistakable scrawl, so much writing that it went over the pictures and spread to the back of the card.

I got time to write because you won't bring any ladies back to this damn trailer for me. Would it kill you to find a nice working girl? Hell, take it out of the budget for my meds. I never paid for it, no, sir, but before I kick off for good I'd trade a handful of them pills for one more hour with a woman who knows what she's doing. How many dying wishes does a man get, for fuck's sake?

As for kicking off, if you are reading this it means I'm gone. That sucks. Not for me though. The part that sucks for me is now. The pain I can deal with. I been busted up before, car wrecks and bar fights. The bad part is the other stuff. Not being able to eat hardly anything or go outside or take a shit by myself. That's no kinda life. Sorry if it pisses you off to hear it, but I'm just about glad it's almost over.

No, the part that sucks will be for you. After. We don't say sentimental shit, never been that kind of family, but I know you'll be missing me at least for a while anyway. Wish I had some advice for you but I don't. Hell, if I'd known how to live a good life and make a pile of money and be like people in the commercials then I would have fucking done it, you know?

And I don't have a will or nothing else for you. That sucks too and I'm real sorry. Been thinking hard and the only thing I have to give you is the picture I have of you as a kid. We don't have no scrapbooks or home movies or trophies sitting in boxes somewhere. Like I said, never been that kind of family. But trust me, you were a great kid, Big Matty. Curious as hell, always laughing, crazy-ass imagination. We hardly never turned the TV on, Cassie and me, you know that? We'd just pop open a couple of beers and sit on the couch and watch you. You probably don't remember none of that. Bad stuff sticks longer than good stuff for some fucked-up reason. But the good times was there. You always thanked me for coming around when you were a kid but you know what? I did it because I liked being around you. My life got pretty messed up sometimes, no lie, and being around you made me feel better. You liked to cut up and carry on and were excited about things. Really.

And you ain't changed as much as you think. I know all teenagers act like assholes because they're going through

a shitty time, and you had it shittier than most. And I
know you can't go back to being exactly like that little kid
again. Nobody does. But you don't want to stay like this
always neither. Some people actually do that, you know. Their
generally a big pain in the ass.

So if you won't bring me a willing woman to warm me
up, then you need to do these things. First, try to forgive
your mom. I know she fucked up but she's been through
a lot. And she protected you from some pretty nasty stuff
when you were a kid.

Second, with me gone you got to start some kinda new
family. I don't mean married and kids and all that mess.
Just like me, you might never do that. Don't matter. But you
need people. Good people. Everybody does. Start with that
sweet girl that's been coming around here. She's been taking
care of our sorry asses so maybe do something for her. It
won't kill you.

And last, get the hell out of here. We stayed here
because we had to, I get that, but it's time for something
different. Tell you what, I'm going to come back as a ghost
in six months and if your still sitting in this trailer with
that surly look on your face I'm going to haunt the shit out
of you. It won't be pretty.

Goodbye.

Uncle Jack

FORTY-ONE

The next day Matt started to take his walks again. When he re-turned in the afternoon, there was only one of the picnic table regulars out at the usual spot, sitting there and having a smoke. He waved Matt over. Matt approached him.

"What's up, my man?"

Matt shrugged. "Nothin' much."

The picnic table regular nodded as if Matt had given an answer. He took a long drag on his cigarette and blew smoke at the sky. "Janice told me about Jack. Sorry to hear about that, man."

"Thanks."

"Jack was a good guy, you know? Cracked me up. Used to come out here and have a beer with us when he was in town. You were just a little shit." He smiled broadly. "Some a the stories he'd tell, you know? Didn't even matter what they was about, just the way he'd tell 'em. Cracked me up." He looked at Matt and his smile faded.

Matt realized that this guy had been part of the trailer park landscape since he could remember. "How long have you lived here?" he asked.

"Forever," the man said, chuckling. He took another long drag on the cigarette. "We lifers, you know? We understand this place." He spread his arms wide, indicating the entire trailer park. "Same deal with Jack. He didn't always live here, but he understood this place, understood us, you know? He was a good guy." The man pulled a crumpled cigarette pack out of his pocket. "You wanna smoke? On me? We'll smoke to Jack."

Matt put up his hand. "Nah. Thanks, though."

"No problem, bro. Take care a yourself."

Matt entered the trailer, but he watched the picnic table man from the window, watched him for a long time. One by one, his buddies rolled out of their trailers and joined him. Smokes were passed around, and somebody took out a bottle. Someone started a game of dominoes and pretty soon they were all laughing and hooting and carrying on.

Matt looked at the clock on the TV. There was still an hour left. He walked out of the trailer and headed toward school.

FORTY-TWO

Mr. Marsh's desk was buried in paper when Matt stepped into his office. He managed to get the surprised look off his face pretty quickly.

"Hi, Matt. It's nice to see you again. Have a seat."

"Thanks."

Matt sat in the chair but didn't say anything. Mr. Marsh collected the papers on his desk, paper-clipping them into neater piles and stacking them up on the shelves beside his desk. "Graduation," he said, rolling his eyes. "I know it's supposed to be the best time of the year—and it is, don't get me wrong—but the paperwork's a beast."

He worked for a few more minutes, then rested his chin in his hand and looked at Matt. "I tried to get ahold of you, you know. After you disappeared. I called every number we had on file for you. I even drove to the address we had listed. I met a lady there said she was your grandmother, but she hadn't seen you in years."

"I'm sorry you wasted your time."

"That's all right. I just wanted you to know you're not alone out there."

"Thanks. I know."

Mr. Marsh gave Matt another quiet minute. "So . . . is there anything I can do for you?"

Matt thought about the question, started to say something, stopped. Finally, he said, "I don't know."

"Well, is there something you need?"

"I don't really know that, either." Matt almost smiled. "That must sound pretty stupid, huh?"

Mr. Marsh smiled for him. "Not at all, Matt. I'm fifty-two years old and I think the exact same thing. All the time."

"Well . . . okay, I haven't really planned this out or anything. But I guess there might be one thing. I know it's a long shot, but do you think I could get another one of those applications from you? Do you think Tech would still take a look at it?"

Mr. Marsh winced. "Oh, Matt, I don't know about that one. Not without a high school diploma. They're pretty firm on that one. I don't think the letters of recommendation would bail you out."

"That's what I thought. But I needed to at least check, you know? I needed to try." He stood up and turned toward the door.

"Not so fast, there, Matt. What are you doing this summer?"

Matt sat back down. "No big plans."

Mr. Marsh riffled through a file, took out a sheaf of papers. "The weeks you've missed put you out of reach for graduation. There's no chance you can walk across that stage next week."

"I know."

Marsh looked at Matt's file. "But you were passing all your classes at midterm. If I can talk to those teachers, get them to give you an incomplete instead of a straight F, you could make up the lost time in summer school. It's six weeks, and you'd need to be there every day and work your tail off." Mr. Marsh studied Matt, who made a keep-going gesture. "But you'd have a diploma by the end of the summer. And maybe we could get those letters to Tech and tell them the diploma is pending."

"Thanks, Mr. Marsh."

Marsh pointed at Matt. "I'm going to give it to you straight, here. If I do all this, I'm putting myself on the line for you. There are people who trust me at Tech. If you drop the ball, it's going to reflect on me, understand? I need to know you're into this. Really into this."

"I want to finish high school."

Mr. Marsh smiled again. "Well, now I know you mean business."

"Why's that?"

"It's the first time I've ever heard you start a sentence with *I want.*" Mr. Marsh stuck out his hand. Matt shook it. "It's a start."

Matt headed for the door, then turned around. "Hey. I guess I want something else."

Mr. Marsh raised one eyebrow. "Really? This must be a big day, Matt. What else do you want?"

"The address of a student. Can you help me find it?"

"Well, now, Matt, you know I can't disclose something like that."

"I get it. Just thought I'd check."

He turned to leave, but Mr. Marsh stood up and turned his laptop around so it was facing Matt.

"But I suppose I *can* tell you that in my experience whitepages.com takes care of anyone not in the Federal Witness Protection Program." Mr. Marsh grinned widely. "Good luck, Matt."

FORTY-THREE

As he walked across town, Matt noticed that the world was still functioning. Even after everything he'd been through. The sun was warming up streets still damp with afternoon rain, cars were driving around, people were talking and laughing. For the first time in weeks, this didn't piss him off quite as much.

He came to a little blue cottage and knocked on the door. The woman who answered was unmistakably Amanda's mother.

The woman just stared at him for a few moments. "You must be Matt," she said.

Oh, shit, Matt thought. He wasn't the kind of guy moms liked to see show up at their door even at the best of times, and he could only imagine what she'd heard about him lately. This was a bad idea. He shouldn't have—

"Oh, you poor thing." The woman reached forward with her flabby arms, wrapped them around Matt and pulled him close to her. "You poor, poor thing." She squeezed him tight and started to sway from side to side a little, like someone trying to put a baby to sleep. Matt should have been embarrassed. But he wasn't.

Finally, she pulled back, but she still held on to Matt, putting her soft hands on either side of his face.

"Amanda has told me everything about you, everything you've been through." She just kept staring at him with that concerned look on her face.

"Yeah." He didn't really know what to say. "She's a talker."

Amanda's mom threw her head back and laughed. "She is, isn't she? Always been a talker, that one."

Matt stood there awhile longer. He cleared his throat. "So . . . is she here?"

Her eyebrows crinkled up. "Oh, she didn't tell you?"

Matt winced. He hadn't given Amanda a chance to tell him much of anything lately.

"She got a callback interview down at the nursing school admissions office. Oh, she was so nervous that she wouldn't let me go with her."

Matt thought about it. "I might go down there, see how she's doing. Do you . . . do you think she'd mind?"

"Of course not! Moms might not always be welcome but teenage boys are another thing altogether, am I right?" She giggled, just like her daughter, and patted Matt on the arm. She hadn't stopped touching him since he got here. But Matt didn't really mind.

"Okay," he said. "I'll head over. It's by the hospital, right?"

"Oh, you can't go without something to eat first. It looks like you haven't had a decent meal in ages. You're skinny as a ferret! You stay there and I'll whip you up something for the road."

"That's okay." Matt took a step backward. "I'd like to get down there right away. So I'm there for when her interview's over, you know? Whether it's good or bad."

Amanda's mom looked surprised, and then her face went from normal to crying in less than a second. She didn't try to hide it or anything. "You're right. You should get down there." She pulled back and wiped her face. "But you come back for a hot meal, you hear? And if you need anything—a ride somewhere or a place to crash or someone to talk to, whatever at all—you come right back here."

Matt nodded and stayed in the doorway for another few moments. "That's really nice. Thank you."

Amanda's mom looked surprised again. And then she started crying again. But she talked right through her crying. "Thank me? Don't be ridiculous." She stepped forward and took both of Matt's hands in hers. "Oh, she would die if she knew I was telling you this, but Amanda used to come home crying, just about every day after school. Those high school kids, they can be so mean. And the cold shoulder, well, that's even worse than the meanness." Amanda's mom shook her head. "But you. Ever since she's met you, she's been okay. No more moping around, sitting in her room by herself. You and that uncle of yours—God rest his soul—gave her a purpose, made her feel useful. Were nice to her. No, Matt, it's me that needs to be thanking you."

She turned him around and nudged him toward the street. "Now get down over there. I'll have dinner waiting for both of you after."

FORTY-FOUR

As Matt neared the hospital he felt that familiar rush of panic. But he kept walking. It only took him a few minutes to find the nursing school entrance.

Amanda came out when he was halfway across the parking lot. Matt spotted the big Buick Electra and cut across to meet her there.

She was fumbling for her keys when she noticed him standing by the car. "Matt!" She quickly wiped her eyes with the back of her sleeve. "What are you doing here?" She looked around the parking lot. "What are you doing anywhere?"

"It was time to get out of that trailer."

They just looked at each other for a little while. "I miss him," Amanda said in a small voice. "I can't imagine what it's like for you, I know it's worse. But I miss him, too, you know?"

Matt took a deep breath. "He would have liked to hear you say that, Amanda." They were quiet for a few more moments. "And I like to hear you say it, too. It helps." He lifted the back-pack he was holding. "The people from After Care gave me a little vase with Jack's ashes. Got 'em right here. Jack never really told me what he wanted me to do with them. But I can't just leave them at the trailer, you know? All cooped up in there. So I guess I need to find someplace to set them free." He looked Amanda in the eyes. "I thought you might be able to help me."

Amanda wrapped Matt in a bear hug. He let her. "I'd love to help you."

Matt stepped back. He cleared his throat and inclined his head toward the nursing school doors. "So what happened?"

Amanda's face crumpled. She started to say something but then stopped. She just looked at the ground.

"What? Wait—they didn't let you in?"

Amanda shook her head slowly.

"That's bullshit. What happened?"

"Oh, you know me. It was a panel interview, and I'm no good with a bunch of people looking at me. People I don't know yet." She sucked in a shaky breath. "I was nervous and awkward, and they said they had some concerns I'd be too timid for the program or to deal with patients." She tried a smile. "It wasn't all bad, though, I swear. They were actually pretty nice about it—encouraged me to do some more volunteer work at the hos-pital, maybe get a job for a year. Then reapply when I have some more experience." She raised both palms. "It's probably good advice, Matt."

"Timid? Are you shitting me?" Matt said. "You're the bravest person I know."

"I'm glad you think so, Matt. I wish you were on the interview panel." Amanda pulled her keys from her purse and unlocked the car door. "Come on. Let's just get out of here."

"No way." Matt started for the entrance.

"What are you doing?"

He turned. "I'm going in there to tell somebody you've already been working as a volunteer nurse these last few months. Available at all hours, calm under pressure, good bedside manner, all that shit. Best nurse I've ever seen. They *have* to let you in."

Amanda wiped her eyes again. "Matt . . . that's sweet. But I don't think it's going to make any difference."

"Fine. If that doesn't work, then I guess I can always beat the shit out of somebody in there."

Amanda looked surprised, then giggled. "That's actually what I felt like doing."

Matt grinned. "Feels good, right?" He walked back to the car, took Amanda by the hand and pulled her toward the entrance. "Come on, we can at least try." They walked toward the front doors together.

ACKNOWLEDGMENTS

This story would not exist without the Writing for Children and Young Adults MFA program at the Vermont College of Fine Arts. VCFA is a place where people are encouraged to take risks, to write something even though it might scare them to do so. It's also a place where people are picked up and dusted off after the inevitable stumbling that comes with attempting to write a novel. A huge thank-you to everyone who helped me with this one in workshop, or who listened to me read from it, or who read it during its various stages and then offered comments and support. With extra special thanks to amazing author and advisor Uma Krishnaswami.

Thank you to my wonderful editor, Phoebe Yeh, and her team, including Elizabeth Stranahan. Phoebe's commitment to getting great stories into the hands of young people is inspiring.

I'm honored that she chose this story and grateful for everything she did to help make it better.

Thanks to my wife, Tracee Mullen Smith, for helping me find my way back to writing. And for everything else. I'm so grateful to be on this ride with her.

The people who work for hospice are incredible, and I can't thank them enough for everything they did during a very difficult time.

The character of Uncle Jack is based on a man named Jerry Perkins. I don't presume to know anything about the afterlife, but wherever he is now, I am sure that Jerry has that mischievous little twinkle in his eye as he makes everyone around him laugh.

Finally, a heartfelt thank-you to the late editor and agent George Nicholson. George believed passionately in this story for many years and is a huge part of the reason that it made its way into the world. He changed my life several times over, and I miss him very much.

ABOUT THE AUTHOR

Clete Barrett Smith is the author of the middle-grade Intergalactic Bed & Breakfast series (*Aliens on Vacation, Alien on a Rampage,* and *Aliens in Disguise*), as well as *Magic Delivery.* A lifelong resident of the Pacific Northwest, Smith taught English, drama, and speech at the high school level while continuing to write. You can follow him on Facebook, on Twitter (@CleteSmith), and online at cletebarrettsmith.com.

About *Mr. 60%,* Clete says, "There are two reasons that I wrote this book. The first was that I helped care for a family member who died of cancer (and just like Uncle Jack in the book, he was a charismatic mess of a guy and I adored him). And the second reason was that I met kids a lot like Matt and Amanda while teaching, and I wanted to tell their story."